THE CHALICE

Behind Blue Eyes: Book 6

SARA J. BERNHARDT

Lavish
Publishing LLC

First Edition

Behind Blue Eyes, book 6

2021 Lavish Publishing, LLC

All Rights Reserved

Published in the United States by Lavish Publishing, LLC, Midland, TX

Cover Design by: Alexcia Productions

Cover Images: CANSTOCK

Paperback Edition

ISBN: 978-1-64900-017-0

www.LavishPublishing.com

Contents

For My Adam

"Vampire issue forth from their graves in the night, attack people sleeping quietly in their beds, suck out all the blood from their bodies and destroy them…"

--John Heinrich Zopfius: Dissertation on Serbian Vampires (1773)

Prologue

SHE WAITED IMPATIENTLY for the sun to sink below the mountains so the night could take her away once more. As she stared out her bedroom window, she watched the romantic twilight darken and stared at each star as they appeared one by one to greet her. *Only a while longer,* she told herself. *Only a while.*

She lay in bed, slowly drifting away. He hadn't come for her, and she wondered if he would ever come again. Would her companion of the night ever come tapping at her window to take her out into the world of darkness, the world that awaits when the sun falls asleep? She knew he was looking for a room with light-colored walls, where a pretty girl lay sleeping with her dark hair shadowing her face from the moonlight spilling in from her window, where a book lay on the nightstand with its place kept by a plastic bookmark. What he found was a room with dark-colored walls, where a tired girl lay sleeping, teddy bear nestled against her breast, where a book lay neglected at the foot of the bed. For some reason, that is the room he had chosen to visit, the girl he had chosen to love.

She awoke tired in the dark. He *had* come back for her. She opened her eyes slowly and smiled before crawling from beneath the warm blankets of her bed and opening the window. A cool breeze rested upon her, making her gasp in delight. She stepped out upon the balcony. The boy didn't speak yet, just led her down the ladder to the grass of her front yard.

"Oh, Victor," she started, but he silenced her.

His hair was the color of the sunlight that he never saw and hung carelessly in front of his face; his eyes were of the deepest amber, where the secrets of centuries were locked away. He was so beautiful that there was no fear within her, only great love and insatiable desire. He held her hand, and they walked along the black, cold streets.

"I have something I want you to see," he whispered.

"What is it?"

"Trust me," he said, resting his forehead against hers.

She leaned in closer, thinking he wanted to kiss her, but he backed away.

"Don't worry," he said. "You'll like this—I promise!"

He pulled a silk handkerchief from his pocket. "So you don't cheat," he said with a smile.

She turned around, allowing him to wrap the scarf over her eyes. He lifted her in his arms and carried her down the streets. It was quiet, with nothing but the sounds of the night; crickets and nightingales sounded in the distance.

Victor at last reached their destination and set her down. He removed the blindfold to reveal a darkened wood.

"Victor—this is amazing."

Even in the middle of the forest, with little understanding of how she had even gotten there, there was no
fear—no suspicion or distrust.

"Wait," Victor said softly. "Do you hear that?"

"Thunder?"

No later than she spoke the word, rain pounded the
forest floors around them—torrents of rain.

Victor smiled. "Dance with me?"

"What?"

"Dance with me."

"I...no..."

"Why not?"

"I...don't know *how* to dance," she whispered,
bowing her head.

"Neither do I. Dance with me."

He took her in his arms, and they danced to the music
of the forest. The rain beat down cold against her skin,
but she didn't feel it. All she felt was the joy of spinning
in Victor's embrace. They danced until colors splashed
the eastern skies, and he took her home.

"Farewell, my dark princess. We'll meet again soon."

He *did* kiss her this time, and she savored every taste
and shudder it sent through her.

"Goodnight, Victor," she whispered, and he was gone.

She met him the next night at the street corner, and they
were silent at first.

"All I wanted was a companion," he said. "Somebody
as a link to the world I left behind. I don't want you to

fear me, but I don't want you to love me either. Please, Emily, forget me—before you become me."

"I want it, Victor," she said, moving her blond hair over her shoulder. "I want it."

"This is no gift, Emily. It's a curse."

"You're leaving, aren't you?"

He nodded. "I told you I was."

"I wasn't sure I believed you."

"I'm moving to Paris—with Daniel—this week. I wanted to bid you farewell."

"Daniel?" She paused, shaking her head. "He did this to you! If you so hate the creature that you have become, then how can you love the one who made you that way?"

"I just—do," he answered. "He's my father, Emily. Please try to understand that."

"You love him?"

"I love him, but I will not do to you what he did to me."

"I want it," she said again.

"When the guilt weighs you down and wearies you to nothingness, will you want it then? When your kind look upon you in horror and hatred, will you want it then?"

Soft tears glistened on her cheeks. "Please, Victor," she whispered. "I need it. I need *you*."

"This is not something to envy, darling."

"But I do. I envy you."

"They all do until they know what it's really like. Then they will envy *you*. How can you stand here this way, offering yourself to me? Do you have any idea what you are trying to make me do? Do you not understand that I can hurt you? That I can *kill* you?"

Her voice rose. "Take me!"

"I cannot bear the thought." He paused, wiping a tear from her cheek.

"I promise I will be good to you. I promise you that this is what I want." She reached for him, but he didn't back away. She held his face in her hands and leaned in for a kiss. She pressed herself against his body and felt his muscles tighten. Her mind flashed with the first time she laid eyes on him. It was a night that would be burned into her memory forever.

She was on her way to the bakery one evening when she saw him, a young man sitting alone in the rain. He was dressed in formal clothing, lacking a jacket and not holding an umbrella. He seemed completely unfazed by the cold.

"Sir?" she questioned, placing her umbrella over his head. "Are you all right?"

"Of course." He stood up, smiling. "Victor Miller."

"Emily Gardner," she replied, grasping his hand. He kissed her hand, and she could tell that his lips were cold even through her gloves. "If you don't mind me asking, why are you sitting in the rain?"

He smiled. "The rain relaxes me. Rain is…exceptionally beautiful." He smiled at her, and heat rushed to her cheeks.

She turned away again, but he stopped her.

"Miss?"

She turned around.

"Do you think you may come by here tomorrow night?"

She smiled. "That depends."

"On?"

"Whether you'll be here or not."

"Yes," he said, laughing, "I'll be here."

"Maybe you'll see me," she answered, "and maybe you won't."

But of course, he did see her the next night and every night thereafter.

She came back to herself, pushing her memories aside. When she looked at him, he was staring through her eyes.

"I remember too, love," he said. "I remember too."

She recoiled, not realizing her thoughts could so easily be read, not realizing he knew what went on inside of her.

"Please, Victor, I don't understand why you cannot love me."

"I do love you, but, Emily, I have loved and lost," he said, his voice quaking as though he fought back tears. "Do you really want to know why I am so in love with the rain? It's something about the feel of it, the smell of it that reminds me of her, and every time the rain comes, I see her face, hear her voice. I can feel her telling me she loves me. Do you really want to become this way? Miserable? Alone?"

She could tell there was more he wanted to say, so she remained silent, staring into his eyes, waiting.

"You are beautiful to me because you are mortal, because you are innocent and do not understand the evil of the world. You are beautiful to me because you are doomed to die someday. If I take you, I take that beauty away."

"I don't care. I want it."

"When your victims look upon you with hate and fear, will you want it then? When you can feel evil within yourself and you cannot stop it, will you want it then? When innocent people weep and scream, begging you for the mercy you cannot give to them, will you want it then?"

"I do! Please, Victor. I love you. I want what you have!"

"What I have?" he yelled. "Don't you understand? There is nothing desirable that I have gained. There is something beautiful that I have lost—my humanity. I can no longer shed human tears or taste human food. I can never grow old with a woman. I can never die and experience the beauty of Heaven. I am a creature of flesh and blood—and only flesh and blood! I am not human, Emily. My only desire is to remain the Victor that I have always been and keep my beloved Anna as my own, but my attempts of bringing her back to me are failing."

She couldn't listen any longer. She couldn't let him keep denying her. Emily drew a small knife from her pocket and, with one more look into Victor's eyes, slashed her wrist. Now he had to take her; now she would have to be his.

"Take me, Victor!"

The blood dripped from her flesh in heavy drops, staining the white concrete.

Victor sighed loudly and turned away. "Do you have any idea what you ask of me? What you are trying to make me do?"

"Take me, Victor!"

His gaze sank into the wound on her wrist. The last

tint of color drained from his face. His veins swelled up like ropes over the contours of his bones and pushed up his pale skin, showing it even whiter. His eyes had lost their fair amber color and had transformed into a disturbing yellow, had become ice cold. He fell to his knees, his muscles quivering as he tried to hold himself back, fighting the hunger surging within him. It was to no avail. He leapt toward her, almost cat-like, licking up what blood he managed to salvage from the dirty sidewalk, only enough to keep himself from killing her.

This time, she ran—ran from the creature she saw him become.

Chapter One

HE SAT THERE, staring at William. "I want you to have this," he said, handing him a leather-bound book.

"You didn't... What she wanted... You didn't, did you?"

"No, William. I couldn't. Do you blame me?"

"Of course not! If ever you were to make her—I would never forgive you."

"I would never forgive myself. One of these days—I will bring Adam back to me, and if your sister were to beg him, I don't know what would happen. You don't want it, do you?"

"No."

"That's good, William. I don't want you to."

"Is your story finished yet, Victor? It seems there should be more."

"There really is no more to tell, but if you desire to know what I had found out in my later years about the life of Daniel, you are welcome to read this." He handed Will a hardcover book and smiled at him.

"What is it?"

"Open it. You will see."

Will opened the book, and instantly a smile spread over his face. He was shocked at first—speechless. "It's… Oh my God, Victor. It's—"

"I found it in my later years, in the Foster house when I was returning Anna's stuffed bear to where I felt it belonged."

"It's the stories of his earlier years, is it not?"

Victor smiled. "His life, my friend. It is Daniel's life, the story of Eric and Thaddeus and all of the pain he endured."

"Thank you," he whispered. "I will take care of it. I promise you."

Victor nodded. "All the answers are there, William. Use them wisely. All the questions about Daniel's life are answered in that journal. Be careful."

"I will."

William closed the journal, with the place kept by a plastic bookmark, and took out his tiny notebook to jot down some notes.

Daniel, child of Eric, and Thaddeus, 1500s.

He sighed and thought for a moment. The words Daniel used, the emotion and description he wrote with— it was hard to believe that people as young as Daniel wrote in such detail in nothing more than a simple diary.

William read the pages with the belief that every word was the unquestionable truth. He sighed, closed the journal, dried his eyes, and, taking a deep breath, sat down at his computer and wrote Daniel's story.

Chapter Two

The life of Daniel Sarcova
Translated by Victor Miller

IT WAS dark when I awoke, and I was taken to the place of my master, whoever he had been. I cannot say whether I was still at home or somewhere far away.

I sadly do not remember my family, only that I had one, but the memories seem as if they are centuries old. I cannot recall names or faces of any kind. It is the year 1522. I don't know where my captors are; all I know is that I am alone in a bed, sheltered from the cold. The room is large, and there are paintings on the walls, one of them the image of a woman on the floor—she is dead. I don't know what these pictures mean, but they frighten me.

It was late when I was taken to this place. I could tell by the sky. I wept openly while my captor held me in his cold, white arms, and he laughed at me tauntingly. I don't know what he wants of me.

His name is Eric, and the man who stood beside him is Thaddeus. They whispered things to each other, but I couldn't understand. They told me that in the evening of the next day, they were going to give me a gift. They said that when I am older, I would understand their gift. It's late, and I have to sleep. I am terrified now of what will happen tomorrow evening when my captors return, terrified of what they may do to me. If this is to be my last entry in this journal, then you know what has happened.

~Leonardo

I awoke from the light after a long rest. It must have been very long; the candles had been lit, and it was evening. I cried out at the sight of my captors looming over my bed with those evil, devilish smiles on their faces. I wish I could tell you what they are, but I can't. They aren't human; I know that for sure. God did not create them.

The man known as Eric stood over me with his black eyes gleaming like a torch, his eyes ageless and filled with untold stories. His companion was horrible—Thaddeus. I felt he was there to harm me. He isn't beautiful like Eric is. He has a long, slender face and a large nose. Though he isn't unpleasant to look at, he isn't a beauty like his companion.

"Be ready, beloved," Thaddeus said, "for the time to come."

Eric nodded in agreement and obedience.

"When I take from this boy what I need, you will be the one to give it back to him."

Eric nodded again. I think he was veiling his uncertainty with his looks of fury and hate. I couldn't see any evil in Eric's face. Eric had frightened me more. It almost seemed as though Thaddeus didn't wish me harm.

Eric leaned in toward me, and I squeezed my eyes shut. I couldn't look into his eyes. They horrified me deeper than I could say, ways that defy description. As my eyes were shut, I thought I felt his breath on my neck. He was moving in closer to me. I was still too frightened to look. As if some inhuman force had attacked me, I felt an incredible piercing sting in my neck. I wanted to yell out, to scream, to weep, and call for help. But I couldn't move. My eyes shot open, and I could see Eric's black hair flung over my face as his animal-like teeth widened a wound in my throat.

There was blood; I could feel it, a lot of it, running from my throat. I knew I was dying.

When at last Eric pulled away from me, he was smiling at me, and I saw his teeth stained and dripping with blood. I was crying, but at the time, I wasn't sure why. Why was Eric drinking my blood?

"I am going to give you a gift," I heard Thaddeus whisper. "Do you want it?"

I couldn't answer. I was in pain. My body burned; my veins felt like sandpaper beneath my skin. My chest tightened, stealing the air from my lungs.

Thaddeus leaned in very close and kissed the top of my head. I tried to nod. I wasn't sure if I had, but I know I had tried repeatedly. I wanted to ask him to save me from Eric, but I saw him bring his wrist to his mouth, then press it to mine. I could feel the incredible heat of his flesh and his blood upon my parched lips. His blood flowed down my throat, and I was able to move now. I suddenly felt strong and warm. Whatever he was doing to me, it didn't matter. I wanted more. I reached up and grabbed his wrist with my hands and drank as fast as I could. I didn't know what was happening to me, why I suddenly had this incredible lust and desire for the taste of blood. All I knew was the pain in my body diminished the more I drank.

"Stop," I heard him whisper.

I locked my mouth harder to his skin.

"Stop."

He yelled at me to cease until he pulled away, practically pulling my teeth from my mouth. It was then the pain returned—more intense than before. I felt as though my body were being ripped in two, as if my insides were being torn from my body.

"Don't fight it," I heard Thaddeus whisper. "Let it happen, and there will be no more pain."

I tried to obey, but the pain was unbearable. I willed myself to remain still and squeezed my eyes shut. I realized he was right; as soon as I stopped struggling and writhing in the bed, there was less pain. When at last it ceased, I felt very tired, but I was thirsty. I wanted for only one thing—blood.

~Leonardo

I think this will be my last journal entry. Last night, Thaddeus and Eric left me in the bed with my body in incredible thirst. I'm in so much pain right now. I don't know what to do. I wept, and my tears were blood that dripped into my mouth, making me scream with the need for blood. It wasn't enough to taste my own; I wanted the blood of Thaddeus as I had before.

This will be my last entry, I fear, for I believe that this illness will destroy me before I have time to understand what it is. I am still just a boy. I know nothing of the world or my place in it.

~Leonardo

I am alone and terrified. I wasn't expecting to wake up again. I thought I would be dead by now. I don't understand what kind of disease my captors have infected me with, but whatever it may be, I know it's not human. It cannot be! The only thing I know right now is that I am not at home. I know that my home is Italy. I can remember that, but here, it is different than Italy. Eric and Thaddeus had spoken to me in words that I understood, but I do not think they came from the same land they had taken me from.

I remembered that Thaddeus and Eric drank blood, and I remembered that feeling I had when I drank it too.

Yesterday, I had a very painful experience. The first thing I learned about this disease is that the sun hurts. The next symptom, I would say, is a desire to hunt. I have these horrible dreams of hunting humans for sport. Satan has cursed me, I am sure. Could there really be another explanation?

I no longer believe that this will be my last entry. Somehow, I know things I have never been told. I know how to hunt and get what I need. Somehow, my captors have released that knowledge into me.

~Leonardo

A single tear fell from his eye as he remembered his sister. The charming Emily, who wanted nothing more than to be with Victor. He shook off the memories and began to think deeper into Daniel's story. It was the year 1522, in the midst of the reign of Vasily III; it was a time when the Muscovite state had expanded, and its rulers were becoming more absolute. William wanted more. He wanted to be there. More than anything, he wanted to see Russia in 1547 under the rule of Ivan the Terrible and witness the conquering of Kazan and Astrakhan. He wanted to know what it was like to live as Daniel had lived, but most of all, he finally understood why Emily had wanted so badly to become immortal. He understood the yearning to experience different centuries and still live on to remember them and speak of them. William wanted to be a vampire.

For three days, he couldn't bring himself to continue the journal; his mind was crowded with the thoughts of Emily, Victor, and his sudden wish to share immortality with them both. During those three days, William didn't speak to Emily, couldn't bring himself to admit that she was right. More than vanity, however, there was fear, for he understood that there may come a time when he would hate what he had become. All the same, he couldn't help but want it.

I searched the streets for blood. It wasn't an easy search. The beggars were dirty and disgusting to me. I couldn't bring myself to touch them. I had no other choice than to sneak into the homes of people, but that didn't always go according to plan. One woman hit me in the back of the head with a frying pan, and a man beat me with his fists. I was too weak to fight back. I was starving, and I realized by a mirror I had found in my room that I looked like a complete terror! That would explain why the women who awoke to find me often fainted or screamed, but even as they lay on the floor, I wasn't given time to prick their neck with my fangs before others came after me.

My skin was white and shriveled, my veins swelled up like ropes, and it hurt to see myself in such a way. I must say that the only reason I was able to recognize my reflection as my own was because the way that I felt was worse!

It's difficult to describe this pain; it's like a dry pulse through every limb of my body. My veins rub together until they are raw. Sometimes it gets so bad that I sink to my knees and hold my breath. I bit into my tongue to hold in the cries of pain and tasted my blood, which brought me to sickness, but the only thing that came from my stomach was blood. Blood everywhere!

I snuck out again, this time sure to keep quieter than the previous times. I snuck through the unlocked window of a bedroom and found a sleeping young woman. Oh, how I wanted her—not her blood, mind you; I wanted her to hold. She was beautiful, stunning, everything I always admired in a woman. Her skin was pale and untainted like porcelain. Her hair shone the brightest of auburn even in the darkness of the room.

I came closer and touched her face. She stirred with a heavy breath that moved the blanket below her breasts. I gasped, backing away, afraid that I may have woken her, but she was still again.

For a moment, I had forgotten entirely about my hunger. It was almost as if I could hear her thoughts. She told me her name was Anya. She said she was lonely. I saw her dreams, saw a boy with hair and eyes like mine. In this dream, she loved him. I knelt beside her bed, stroking her hair and watching her dreams play out. It was the strangest thing. I did not understand how any of it was possible, but nor did I care.

This disease was nothing how I imagined when Thaddeus had first infected me. More than painful symptoms were some incredible abilities. As I stared at the sleeping beauty before me, I thought only of how I wished I could be that boy she rested there dreaming of.

The night was cold, so I pulled the blanket higher, covering her shoulders. I wished I could watch her wake beneath my touch, but I knew that because of the way I looked, I would do nothing but frighten her. I ran my fingers through her scarlet locks of hair; it felt like silk in my hands. I touched her face again, feeling the softness of her skin—like the petals of a rose. I could feel her blood pumping beneath her flesh; I could taste the salt of her skin in my mouth. My heart begged for her life, and I knew I should leave before my hunger destroyed her. My body was screaming at me, telling me to sink my teeth into her neck. I pulled my hand away from her face, kissed her forehead, and departed on my way "home" or whatever the place my captors had taken me would be called.

Through the darkness, I had turned with fear several times, sure that there had been somebody there, but all I saw were damp cobblestones. I gazed up at the frost-covered roofs and shivered. I realized the air should have felt colder to me—perhaps I had a fever. I spun around again, feeling the presence of somebody behind me. I sped up my pace until I came to the place my captors had taken me—the mansion. I went to my chambers, sat in bed, and wept. My tears were blood that dripped through my fingers, staining the beautiful blankets. I'm frightened, and I want to go home—to the family I can't remember.

~Leonardo

The nights are long. I at last got to feed. I ripped open the neck of a woman with silvered hair. The blood was the liquid life that replenished my beauty and made me whole and strong again. I cannot recall how many nights have passed since last I wrote, but the presence that I felt following me that night is upon me every second! I can feel the ground tremble beneath me. I can hear the faint sound of a heartbeat. I think it is the Lord mocking me for my sins, reminding me of my possible damnation. I weep like a child every night. I shed burning, scalding tears—and I am hungry again.

I hunted again last night but was tortured and nervous at the feeling of that presence again, so tormented and frightened that I returned early without a single drop of blood to satisfy my hunger. I tried to sleep, but even as I lay in bed, I could feel the presence of somebody as if they stood right beside me, and I couldn't close my eyes for several hours.

By the time I was finally able to rest, it was near

dusk. Something terrifying yet miraculous occurred. I was awakened, not by the sound of that heartbeat but the feeling of it against my chest, an anti-rhythm of my own. My eyes were slowly opened because I was not afraid this time; there was a sense of comfort here. I wanted to fall back asleep, humming the tune of that familiar heartbeat that had been haunting me for weeks. The face that met my eyes when I opened them didn't cause me to yell out in terror but more to stare upon in confusion and awe. There was a faint light that emanated from his flesh. I was being cradled in the arms of a man who felt hard and cold—the same way that Eric and Thaddeus had—but for some reason, I did not think he was one of them. I thought I was being held in the arms of a white, stone statue, his features carved by Heaven's light itself. He smiled at me, and I let out a soft mortal yell and scrambled from his arms, quickly covering myself with the blankets of my bed. He laughed almost silently, as if it were only meant for himself.

"Don't be frightened," he told me. "Eric and Thaddeus are children of mine. This house they have taken you to is mine, the clothes they have given you, the wine they let you drink, all of it is mine, Leonardo—all of it."

I jumped back with a gasp, his voice tang and echoed like something from a dream. In this angelic voice, he had said my name. *Leonardo*.

"You don't have to be frightened of having nowhere to go now, my wounded darling."

Perhaps he was a ghost, a beautiful phantom—maybe an angel.

"You will be safe here," he continued, "and do not ask

me how I know your name. I have been watching you, Leonardo. You have much to learn."

It took me a long moment before I was able to speak, and still, when I did, it was a choked whisper.

"Wha—what—what are you?"

He laughed silently. "The same thing you are—flesh and blood."

"Flesh and blood?" I whispered.

"Yes," he answered, "flesh and blood—but not human."

His words caused me to recoil in more than confusion but actual terror.

"Although you are not human any longer, there are human needs you still possess, Leonardo."

"What needs are those?"

"My name is Ashman," he said, "and that is all you will ever need to know about me. Ashman the Great, I was once called."

I couldn't speak yet.

"The things that you need, my wounded one, are a companion and a teacher. You don't want to be alone, my love. You have a human heart and a human desire for companionship—do you not, Adorato?"

"I do."

I loved the way he spoke to me—so softly. He speaks to me in Italian, as I know he must, since I can understand him and cannot understand the Russian peasants I kill when they curse me! He made me feel as if my very father stood there embracing and comforting me. So, there are others out there like me—thank God! So, I wasn't so alone after all; so I wasn't the only one.

~Leonardo

Chapter Three

HE MOVED in the most unnatural ways; he seemed to float when he walked, and each movement was like stone transforming into silk or something liquid. He told me I was a blood-hunter like him and that I am immortal. He also told me that since my own blood wasn't given back to me, I was weak. I was supposed to be given Eric's blood, mingled with my own, but I was not. It does not grieve me to know that because of this, I cannot create others like myself.

Ashman told me he is my master now and that he will teach me all I need to know—including how to speak Russian.

"You are hungry, Leonardo."

"I am, Master. Very hungry."

"You can drink from me, beloved."

I took a step closer and closed my teeth around the pumping artery in his neck. I bit down and succeeded with two punctures. When I heard him gasp, I backed away.

"It's all right," he whispered, moving his black hair from his neck. "You can bite harder."

I bit as hard as I could into his cold flesh and heard him moan.

"Keep drinking," he whispered.

I didn't hesitate again; I drank as fast as I could. His body stiffened, and I feared I was hurting him, but I couldn't stop. The blood felt so good pouring into me, and I locked my mouth and bit deeper. He seemed to falter, unsteady on his feet, and I forced myself to stop.

"You have wonderful self-control, Adorato." He chuckled. "But you weren't hurting me."

I sucked a drop of blood from my bottom lip and bowed my head.

"You can look at me, Leonardo, and you can take more if you desire it."

"You know I do."

He laughed. "I do."

~Leonardo

I awoke to Ashman beside my bed, and I gasped, noticing his pointed teeth when he smiled, realizing mine were like that too. I ran my tongue over my teeth and instantly tasted my own blood, but the wound had healed so quickly it seemed as though it had never really been there at all. Ashman leaned in toward me and brushed his lips across my neck. My memories flooded back, and I felt the prick of Eric's teeth as if it were happening again. My eyes burned with unshed tears.

"Don't weep, Leonardo," I heard my master whisper

kindly in my ear. "I'm not going to hurt you, and I'm not going to leave you either."

Something about the way he spoke told me I could trust him.

He leaned in closer and pierced my skin with his teeth. I gasped from the pain, and he pulled away before taking blood.

"Did I hurt you, Adorato?"

"Yes," I answered quietly, "but I am inclined to ask you to do it again."

He chuckled and bit down into my neck again. There was pain, but with the pain was this incredible feeling of passion, an orgasmic sensation of—love, maybe. I didn't want him to stop.

When at last he let go, I felt as if he had taken all my strength and wakefulness with my blood.

He lifted me from the bed. "I have something to show you. I'll take you there."

He carried me to a back room and pulled back the silk rug. Beneath was a door. He carried me down stone steps, lit by torches on the walls.

Ashman must have mastered the skill of sculpting. There were statues everywhere, carved from white stone —some of the virgin and the child of God, which he told me about. Others were of a beautiful Egyptian woman, Egyptian like him. He must have loved her because of the way she always seemed to be reaching out to him. He stood there staring at the statue as if she could speak.

He told me the religious icons were meant to remind me to scowl at the Lord for letting us become this way and then damning us.

"The Lord hates us and this woman here," he started,

pointing to the beautiful Egyptian statue. "I don't want you to ask me a single question about her."

He terrified me when he spoke so forcefully. His power was beyond any possibly imaginable, and I feared him almost as much as I loved him.

Many days passed, and my understanding of Ashman grew. He has lived for many centuries, and those centuries brought him his power. I can't even comprehend what I am—a creature forced to feed off the blood of humans and also be gifted with incredible abilities, such as the gift to read the thoughts of mortals and move at a speed no mortal eyes could follow. It is an amazing transformation. I am protected now by my immortality, by my damnation. I love what I am. I am powerful and rich beyond my deepest desires and fantasies. Ashman protected me, and I must confess, as much as I am growing to love him, he can be cruel.

He took me back to the home of that girl whose dreams I had watched. Before that, he let me tear open the throat of a man he found asleep in a nearby house. I tried to leave him unconscious, but I couldn't stop drinking. Ashman told me the slight emotions of mortal guilt that I have should leave me soon.

When he took me back to the home of that pretty girl, he told me he wanted me to take her.

"I would love more than anything to take her, Master, but I can't."

"And why can't you do such a thing, Leonardo?"

"Because I haven't the strength. Not without your help."

"Why do you say this, Leonardo?"

"Because I haven't the strength. You told me yourself. I haven't the strength to create *any*."

A silent laugh shook through him. "I didn't ask you to make her, Adorato. I asked you to take her."

"I don't understand."

"Take her, beloved. Cradle her in your arms as though you love her."

"Oh, I would love very much to do that, Mast—"

"Then take her blood into yourself and let her die in your embrace."

"What?" I choked out. "Die? But, Master, I cannot watch such a girl die."

"And just why not?"

"Because, Master…because—"

"She is beautiful to you because she is mortal. You fancy her innocence and her youth. She is beautiful to you because she is doomed. Take her, Leonardo. You must!"

"I can't, Master."

He didn't say anything, but his eyes hardened.

"Please—I won't. I refuse."

"If you do not do it, Adorato—I will."

My eyes burned with unshed tears. "Why, Master? Why are you doing this to me? I don't wish to hurt her. I don't want to kill her."

"But you will, Leonardo."

"No!" I yelled. "No—I will not."

"You will!"

"No." I pointed behind me. "I will not enter that house if you are only going to make me murder her."

"You will do it, Leonardo, because I am telling you to."

"I can't."

"You fancy her, Leonardo, because she is mortal."

"No, Master. I fancy her because she is beautiful."

"You must understand," he started slowly, "that we must kill without care and always remain in the shadows."

"So, I can never have her?"

"Not unless you intend on killing her, beloved. Not unless you have the will to take her into your arms and let her die."

"Then I cannot know her…because I will not kill her. You told me if I didn't, you would. So kill her if you must, but I will not watch because I don't have the power to stop you."

"I don't want to kill her, Leonardo," he whispered.

"What?"

"I don't want to kill her," he repeated loudly. "I want *you* to do it. I want you to learn. You need a teacher, my love. You have confessed you don't want to bear this burden alone, and on my immortal life, I have sworn to lead and protect you, Adorato—TAKE HER!"

"I will not!" I yelled. "I will not!"

"If I have to drag you kicking and screaming, you will."

I shook my head dramatically.

He growled under his breath and grasped the hood of my blue cloak. "Go, Leonardo!" he screamed, pushing me forward. "Go!"

"I won't!"

"I don't have all night to argue with you, Leonardo," he snarled angrily, "nor all night to punish you."

I scowled at him.

"So, tomorrow night, we will return to this place, and if you do not enter—then we will see."

He dragged me down the cold cobblestones by my hood. I thought silently, trying my very hardest to conceal my thoughts. *I will run away—tonight—before the master rises. I will run to anywhere that will keep that perfect girl from harm. I am leaving, and I'm taking Anya with me.*

I continued to sigh and snarl as he dragged me, stumbling as if I were a mortal boy.

"You are a mortal boy to me!"

"Yes, Master, and you are a monster!"

He threw me down and struck me hard across the face to the point I wept. He looked at me, and I saw a painful expression in his eyes.

"I'm sorry, Adorato. I shouldn't have struck you. If you were mortal, I would have taken out your teeth with that strike."

I touched my throbbing cheek and realized I was bleeding. The pain had ceased because of my new power, but there was still blood that came off on my fingertips, and I stared at my shaking hand. I stumbled to my feet, and Ashman extended his hand to touch me.

"Adorato."

I stepped back so quickly I fell.

"Leonardo," he whispered.

He leaned down, and I rested my head upon my drawn-up knees, but when he touched me, he didn't hurt me. He lifted me in his arms.

"I told you I was sorry," he whispered. "I should not have struck you."

I loved hearing his so inhuman voice, despite the

words. Regardless of what he felt he needed to tell me, I loved to listen to him. The unnatural ring in his voice made me sleepy, as if his simple words were a lullaby. I didn't fall asleep in his arms, though I wanted to; it wasn't until he set me gently in my bed that I slept.

As much as Ashman captivates me and as much as I feel I love him, I still cannot let him hurt beautiful people. I will run away tomorrow, and I will take Anya with me.

~Leonardo

Ashman is stronger than I gave him credit for; perhaps I *am* just a foolish boy. Last evening, I awoke, bound to the posts of my bed. I began squirming in the sheets and yelling. Ashman woke (or maybe hadn't been asleep) and came into the room.

"I couldn't let you run away," he said. "I know what will happen to you, Leonardo."

"I won't let you hurt her!"

"Why are you so protective of her? Why *her,* Adorato?"

"She dreams of me!" I yelled, pulling my wrist loose. "She dreams of me."

He grabbed my wrist and tied it tighter to the post.

"Stop this, Leonardo. My blood has given you more strength than I intended. Do not use it against me!"

"I refuse to let you hurt her."

"Why? Why do you fancy her so dearly?"

"SHE DREAMS OF ME!" I demanded.

"How do you know? How can you be so sure it is you?"

"It is me! The Lord allows me to see her dreams—shows me it is me who she dreams of."

He laughed loudly, and it startled me. "The Lord? What Lord is that, Leonardo?"

I didn't respond.

"The one who hates us? The one who condemns us? Never speak of God again, Leonardo, or I will strike you harder than I did before."

"Why?"

"Because you need to listen to me, and that is what I told you."

"Don't hit me, Master. Please don't hit me."

"I'm not going to hit you, Leonardo, but you will lie here, bound to the bed for as long as I feel is necessary. And you listen to me, boy. Whatever I say is what you have agreed to learn, and whatever I tell you to do is the same. You *will* obey."

I scowled at him and struggled to free my wrists, but it was too painful. I hated not being able to move. I hated feeling powerless and weak. It was driving me mad. I would do almost anything to be untied. I lay there and screamed, hoping I would anger Ashman either enough to cut the bounds or even come in and scold me—even hit me. But he left me all alone—ignored my cries until I began to weep apologies. Only then did he let me go.

I couldn't decide what it was that Ashman felt for me —love or duty. One day he was telling me all the things I would ever need to know to be safe and happy, and the next, I awake tied to the posts of my bed after he tried to force me to kill a girl I feel passion for. Perhaps Ashman was right. Perhaps she is beautiful to me only because she is mortal.

Then why do I feel such a deep, intense need to protect her from all harm? To make sure nobody touches her except me? Why do I not wish to kill her?

Ashman called me a coward. He told me I was weak, that I love too much. I don't understand myself; I don't understand why I cannot kill her. I am Leonardo. I am the child of Ashman The Great. I am no coward! That is all I must prove—to Ashman and to myself. I am no coward.

I think I should take her in my arms and let her die in my embrace; I would love to, wouldn't I? I am a strong, beautiful blood hunter. Ashman told me that. I can take the beautiful Anya, for she loves me, and I deserve her. I think if I kill her, I wouldn't be trapped by her beauty. I cannot get her out of my head. I cannot think about anything but her. Perhaps I need to kill her, simply to free myself from her spell. Perhaps I need to kill her to learn what it is Ashman wants me to learn. Perhaps I *will* kill her. Ashman would be pleased with me.

"You do," Ashman told me softly. "You do deserve her."

"So, I can take her…tonight, Master?"

"Tonight."

He took me out again. "Don't make a sound, Adorato."

I nodded. Through the window, we entered, and there was Anya, sound asleep, dreaming of her missing love. Her scarlet locks shadowed her face, but I could still see she was beautiful. Yes, this beauty deserved to die with my fangs in her throat; her life deserved to be mine.

Ashman left me alone. He said he would wait outside for me.

I slowly lifted her head from the pillow so gently that

not even a heavy breath escaped her lips. Her pale skin was flawless; I couldn't help but caress her face. I did feel hunger but not for her blood. I felt…hot, almost sore with the need to hold her—to hold her so close. I couldn't be any closer. I could feel the warmth of her blood beneath her flesh, the flesh I was meant to tear into to get to the life beneath it, to drink it up until there was no more need.

I loved her.

I pressed my lips to her neck and kissed it over and over as if she knew I was there—as if she was waiting for me to tell her I loved her.

I knew she couldn't understand my language, nor could I understand hers, but when I whispered "I love you" in Italian, I saw a sleeping smile spread across her face. I saw her dreams. She was dreaming of me again. Well, not me, perhaps, but the boy who looks like me and speaks like me—the boy who would love her like me if ever I were given the chance. I thought it best to take her when she dreamed so she would die in peace—murdered by the boy she loved. As I tasted the salt of her flesh, my teeth sank before I had time to stop them. I instantly tasted her blood as a burst of relief from my painful hunger passed through me. *I have self-control,* I told myself. *Ashman told me that. Don't give in to it, Leonardo. Control it. CONTROL IT! She is too beautiful to die. What was I thinking?*

I pulled away, leaving her unconscious. I wasn't sure how hard I had bitten her, but I knew she was alive. I kissed her softly, letting my tongue slightly pass between her parted lips.

I left the house to see Ashman there waiting for me. I

made sure he saw the tiny pin drops of blood on my chin, and I forced a synthetic smile.

"Deception, deception." He sighed. "You cannot fool me, boy." But he wasn't angry; he was smiling!

I bowed my head.

"Look at me, Leonardo."

I obeyed.

"I see the look in your eyes now, my child. I see the love that your dark eyes show me, Leonardo. If I must, I will let you keep her alive, but you must promise me now, Adorato—you *will* remain in the shadows!"

"So never can I even speak a word to her, Master?"

"No, Leonardo. I see your desire to protect her, to not let another near her, to not let another touch her, but—"

"She dreams of me, Master."

He leaned in and embraced me warmly. He felt like a huge chunk of stone, like one of his statues, but I loved it.

"She is mortal, Leonardo."

"Yes, but may I change that?"

"Here is another thing I am meant to teach you—no."

"But why?" I asked. "If we do not make her like us, then she will...well, then she will die."

"Yes. Yes, she will. But she will also live."

"But—"

"She is not meant to become like us, my love. We cannot populate the world with our kind. It is not meant for everyone, Adorato. I don't even believe it was meant for you. Your mind was not filled with the knowledge of our kind as it should have been, and even if you were to teach her about it, she would only hear your words as the ravings of a madman. You cannot be free from me,

Leonardo. Let her go, and someday, you may understand and be able to lead your own life.

"There may come a time when hatred for the blood befalls them, Leonardo, a time when they hate what they are. You cannot give this blood to all who meet you. They can't all be given this gift of darkness, child."

I bowed my head. "I understand." And I did understand. As sad as it made me, I understood it completely.

Ashman told me I try too hard to please him.

"Don't be afraid of me," he said. "Be my challenger, Leonardo. Question me if you wish."

"You know I love you."

"Yes. Listen to me now. You can walk the streets of the city later if you wish, but your body will always tell you when the sun is coming, and then you must be sure you are safe from the violent rays of daylight."

"I understand," I said. "I don't want to be afraid of you, Master, but neither do I want—"

"I will never strike you like that again, Leonardo —never."

"Never?"

"Never. I love you too, child."

I smiled and saw his eyes flash in the most unnatural way I had ever seen. Were his eyes glowing in the darkness like a nocturnal predator in the woods? What frightened me more was if they were, then mine were too.

"Master, what...? What are we?"

Ashman smiled. "Flesh and blood. It doesn't matter what you are. You are more human than you are monster."

I sighed and nodded.

"It is early in the night still," he said, turning from the

uncomfortable subject I had started. "I have put this off for too long."

"What?"

He chuckled. "Russian lessons. Come along now."

He led me to the room where he first began my teachings of our kind and started teaching me the language he felt I needed. I don't understand why he wanted me to learn how to speak Russian. I am not supposed to speak to anyone anyway. I guess it doesn't matter. I do as I am told.

It has actually been months since last I wrote, and my master has been teaching me Russian constantly. It has not been easy.

For the past few nights, I had disobeyed my master. I snuck out after dark to visit my Anya. The first night was beautiful. I knelt beside her bed and watched her dream. I knew she was reaching out to that boy to find he was not there. Several times, she reached out in her sleep, and I held myself back, controlled myself from taking her hand in mine, waking her from her rest, and bringing her into my arms. Not many more times was I able to resist it. She reached out her delicate hand; her white, shimmering, untainted skin was enough to bring me to her side. I slowly moved my hand to meet her soft fingers and squeezed them in my palm. She woke slowly under my touch to meet a gentle smile. She gasped and pulled her hand away.

I put my finger to my lips. "Why are you frightened?" I whispered. I reached out to her, and her fear diminished as I twisted a strand of her crimson hair around my fingers.

"Daniel?"

"What?"

"It is you…the boy—the boy from England who has found his way into my dreams."

I smiled.

"Is it not you?"

"Of course it is me. Why do you say England?"

"Is it not England?"

"Oh, my darling," I whispered softly. "Think…Italy."

"Italy?"

"Mmm…yes, Italy."

I opened my arms, and she fell into them, weeping openly.

"No tears, Anya," I said. "Never again will you be forced to awake to find you are alone." I hoped she didn't notice the way I spoke. I am still not very good at Russian.

"Is it really you?"

"Would you like to find out for yourself?"

She nodded.

I took a step closer and put my hand on her cheek. I touched my lips to hers and kissed her the sweetest way I could. When I pulled away, she was smiling.

"It *is* you," she whispered, locking her crystal eyes on me.

And that night, both of us realized that whether by fate or not—we were in love.

The next night when I came for her, she was awake.

"You came."

"You waited."

"Of course I waited. I've been waiting all the years of my life, Daniel."

I loved the way she called me Daniel. It was a name used by her and her only, a name she loved because she loved me. I kept the name Leonardo to myself—the name I hated the very sound of, the name that made me see myself as an arrogant, misbehaved child. I hated that name.

Once again, I spent the night making her dreams come true one by one. I wish I could have told her that I am not human. I wish I could have told her my only human qualities are my body and my blood, but of course —I could not. I stared into her eyes one last time and left her before sunrise.

"Will I see you tomorrow?"

I nodded.

"Must I wait until dusk?"

I touched her cheek, and she smiled. I left her after a soft kiss on the cheek.

I returned silently to my chambers until Ashman awoke me the next evening.

"I haven't seen you the past two nights, Leonardo. Where have you been?"

"Out alone," I said, rolling over.

"Open your eyes, boy!"

I sighed and sat up with a yawn. "I got hungry."

"You know you are not supposed to hunt alone yet, and don't lie to me, boy. I can tell by your color that you have not fed enough."

"What are we?"

"Flesh and blood."

"Master, why do you torment me with that phrase? What are we?"

"Why are you so angry?"

"She dreams of me, Master!" I screamed, throwing my hands up. "She dreams of me."

He sighed. "Leonardo—"

"Tell me what we are. Tell me why I cannot be with her, why she cannot be one of us. Tell me, Master! Why can't I love her?"

"There are no answers, Leonardo!" He stepped forward, and pointing an angry finger at my chest, he continued. "A blood hunter is what you are, strong and immortal. You will want to make them all, Leonardo, but you can't."

"My name is Daniel! That is my name now!"

"You are a fool! You live in her dream world, boy. You must remain in the shadows, away from the mortal world. As the pupil you are meant to be, you must obey me. If you wish to be on your own, you will never survive!"

"There are answers, Master. I know there are. How is it you know nothing about this cruel life of darkness you have had personally inflicted on you and now have inflicted on me as well?"

"We are what we are, and whatever that happens to make us—so be it. That is all there is to tell you, Leonardo. You must go to Anya tonight. You must tell her it's over."

My eyes welled with tears, but I refused to let them fall. "Why?" It was all I could say.

"I have told you where your place is and what would happen if you didn't listen. I allowed you to let her live.

That was very generous of me. That will change if you do not end it. End it, Adorato, or I will kill her myself."

I couldn't fight the tears anymore, and they flowed freely. "Why are you tormenting me? Why do you wish to cause me pain?"

He embraced me. "Your place is in the shadows."

"I can't do it, Master! What will I tell her?"

"Tell her you can't love her. Tell her—you *don't* love her, Adorato."

I just stared.

"I love you, which is why I chose to take care of you —to rescue you. I would never do anything to cause you pain, no matter what it may be. I would never do anything to hurt you. You must do this. Someday, you may understand why. This is not a punishment. I can teach you not to care. I can teach you to be without regret and pain, but you must obey me, Leonardo. No more of this."

I didn't know how to respond. I wiped my eyes with the back of my hand and looked away. "I can't do it, Master! There is no way I can bring myself to let her go."

He sighed. "Leonardo, we've been through all this. I can teach you not to care."

"Then teach me, Master!" I yelled, falling back into his embrace. "Teach me."

~Leonardo

Chapter Four

I WENT to Anya that night. She was sitting up in bed, smiling. I refused to let myself return the gesture.

"Are you all right?" Her voice was like a bell choir. Lord, how I loved her, how I still love her.

I didn't know what to say at first, but I was sure she recognized the awkwardness of our meeting. She leaned in to kiss me, but I moved aside.

"Daniel...?"

Daniel. "I—Anya..."

"Daniel, what is it?"

I sighed. "I shouldn't be here. I need to leave, Anya. I'm sorry." I was frantic, terrified Ashman would become impatient and hurt her. I was scrambling to leave and couldn't get out fast enough.

"Daniel, wait!" she called. "Please—wait!"

I turned back to her, but then I heard Ashman's voice in my head. *"Do it, boy."* I cried out, startled. I turned around, trying to find him, but the room was empty, save for Anya, who stood in terror and concern. Her face was wet with tears, and I hated myself for it.

"Daniel, please!" she called out again. "What's wrong with you?"

"I'm sorry," I answered, pushing her away. "I can't love you!"

She was stunned, stricken completely dumb for a moment. "What?" she choked out. "Why are you saying this? What's wrong? Please talk to me."

"I'm sorry," I repeated, stepping back again. "Not by your will or mine, it has to end. I cannot be with you. I'm sorry, darling!"

"Daniel, there's something terribly wrong. Tell me what it is. Is it Ashman?"

I froze. "Ashman?" I whispered. She hadn't heard me. "It's Ashman," I said a little louder, calming a bit. "Yes, it's Ashman."

"Daniel, it's all right. When you are free of him, we can be together."

"Anya, you don't understand. I will never be free of Ashman, and so we can never be."

"Why are you saying this? Daniel, please. I don't understand what you are telling me."

I kept turning my face away from her, refused to look into her eyes.

"After dreaming of you my entire life, I finally find you, and now you are leaving me?"

"No, Anya. I am not who you think. Keep dreaming, Adorato, Keep dreaming."

"Daniel!" She was crying, and her screams were choking out her words. "Daniel!"

I ran as fast as I could from her house and back home,

where I fell into Ashman's arms the way a young mortal would have.

"You did what you needed to do, Adorato. You know it's good."

"I am ready for you to teach me how to not care!"

"First come some other things, my blood child. Just be patient, Leonardo. Everything will come to you all in good time."

I nodded, looking at the floor.

He lifted my chin. "It's all right. You know I love you."

The first things Ashman has been teaching me are the truths about our kind; he began the very next evening.

"Now," he started, "putting Anya out of your mind, I will begin your teachings."

I nodded.

"What we are, Leonardo, doesn't matter. I have told you before. The only thing I can tell you is we are immortal blood hunters."

"I do love the idea of everlasting life, Master. Although I may not understand it, and as much as I hate Thaddeus and Eric for what they did to me, I love them for what they have given me."

"That may soon change," he answered, "and although you are said to be immortal, there are still things that can destroy you."

"Like the sun?"

"Yes, the sun and the sustained heat of fire. That is the only thing that can truly hurt you."

"But still—why can I not make Anya?"

"Put her out of your mind, Leonardo!"

"I do not mean to make you angry. I am only trying to understand."

"I told you. It takes a great deal of strength to become one of us, which I do not see in her. We are a secret species, Leonardo. Our secrets must be kept from mortals."

"I understand," I answered, even though I didn't entirely. "Anya will forever be bound in my dreams, Master?"

He sighed. "Enough of that. Put her out of your mind, Leonardo."

I nodded.

"Now listen to me. You may love and possibly adore the comfort of your own bed, but it is not our way."

"Our…way?"

"Our way is the way of the master, Leonardo."

Because of the strange look in his tense eyes and the slight raise of the eyebrows, I knew he could not have meant himself, so I asked him.

"What—master?"

He smiled. "*Our* god, Leonardo—the one who loves us for what we do. The one who gave us our power."

"But you had said that…God and…the Lord—"

"They hate us, Leonardo, hate us for what we do. They condemn us, and they damn us. Listen to me, boy— the one true master is *not* God."

I fell dumb for a moment, confused. I knew what he was saying. I was sure I understood, but I wanted him to tell me, so I asked him again.

"Say the name, Master."

He smiled—the way Eric would have—and although

it did not frighten me, it made me sad. He leaned in close to where I could see the monster in him, could see how inhuman he really was.

"Say the name, Master!" I demanded.

His eyes began to tint to a yellow, almost reddened in color. The blood in him appeared living as it flushed his cheeks and lips. He chuckled, and his teeth appeared to be evil beings of their own. The voice in which he said the name was not his own but the voice of a monster, a madman; it was not my Ashman who spoke to me.

"Lucifer!" he said. "Lucifer!"

I stumbled backward. His face was distorted with this new ghastly look of evil. Ashman the Great, ancient Egyptian pharaoh, now looked more monstrous than ever before. *Lucifer, Lucifer, Lucifer.*

I fell to the floor, my lip trembling and my blood tears devouring my vision. I watched as Ashman's features softened, and he looked once again like the man I knew. I recoiled, wondering if what I had seen was real.

He sighed. "You can cry, Leonardo," he said to me kindly, "but this is the last time." He knelt before me, and I backed up. "I'm not going to hurt you. I am sorry I frightened you."

I slowly crawled toward him on my knees, and he held out his arms to accept an embrace. I was hesitant, but as soon as I felt his arms around me, I was safe and warm again. I wept for only a few moments and only because he told me I could.

"Weep for a long time, Adorato," he said, "for it will be for the last time."

And I did. I wept for Anya and Thaddeus. I wept for the poverty in Russia and the unwanted beggars I had killed to satisfy my thirst. I wept for the misery my monstrosity has brought and for the family I cannot remember. I wept in his arms until I cried myself dry and was hungry again.

He raised his wrist to his mouth and bit down. He pulled back without a single sign of pain, breaking the veins and tendons, tearing his beautiful shimmering skin. He let the blood pour into my mouth and fill my empty bloodstream. When he pulled away from me, I watched the wound heal layer by layer, and his skin was beautiful and untainted again. I couldn't help but smile. He helped me to my feet.

"Choose your finest," he said, but the tone in his voice made it sound unauthentic, as though he wanted to say something else.

I stared blankly for a moment and looked at him, confused. I watched his expression change rapidly when he chuckled.

"Don't look at me that way," he said kindly. "Choose your finest, Leonardo. We are leaving."

"Leaving?" I cried. "When? Where?"

"Do not ask questions," he told me, putting his hand on my shoulder. He stared into my red-filmed eyes and watched my eyebrows wrinkle together. "Don't weep. It will be all right. Just do as I say."

I nodded.

"No need to burden yourself with common possessions. Choose only your most adored treasures."

Although many frightening things had taken place in this house, I was born here; I was created in this house. I didn't want to leave. I wanted to keep the comfort of my own bed and the essence of Thaddeus. I wanted to remember without trying. I wanted memories to flood back to me when I noticed specific details of my home where so many things had happened.

I chose my most beautiful clothes and some of the jewels that Thaddeus left for me. I brought along one of the blankets from my bed that reminded me of Ashman and brought back the kind voice of Thaddeus. I sank into my mind, remembering my captors. I wondered why Eric had been so cruel to me when his companion was so kind. I put them out of my mind and let Ashman know I had everything I needed.

"One more night, my love," he told me. "Savor the comfort of your bed for the last time."

I nodded, still uncertain but too afraid to question. I love the feeling of letting my limbs fall into place at random, in the most comfortable positions, as I fall asleep listening to the beating of my master's heart.

The next evening, Ashman woke me very early, when the sky was still blue. We gathered our things and left the house. I looked back several times with intense longing.

"Come on, Leonardo," Ashman whispered solemnly.

We walked for a long time until we came to a burial ground. It was quiet there—no beggars asking for food, no impoverished people sleeping on the ground. The graves were old and hadn't been tended to.

"Come now, Adorato. This is our new home."

"What is, Master? There is nothing here."

"Look *deeper,* Leonardo."

He knelt down and brushed a few inches of loose soil from the ground. Within minutes, he had uncovered a wooden board. "We will venture beneath, Leonardo, like Lucifer."

I only stared, perplexed.

He lifted the board—it was a door. I was hesitant; I was confused and utterly frightened. He closed the door behind him and walked down stone steps into darkness.

A man appeared before us. I gasped and clung to Ashman's cloak. The man was tall with a beautiful mane of black curls and black eyes.

"Who dares enter?" he growled.

His anger startled me. Ashman smiled.

Instantly, the man's face lost all emotion and became rock hard. He whispered, seemingly choked with shock. "Ashman?"

My master smiled again. Did he know this man?

"It cannot be." The man dropped to his knees, bowing as if to royalty.

"Look at me, Alexander."

The man stood to his feet with only a few thin tears staining his cheeks. My master opened his arms—as he had for me. He took one more step toward the man. Alexander froze for a moment, seemingly trying to decide if his eyes were deceiving him. He took one clumsy, mortal step toward my master and fell affectionately into his arms.

"How can it be?" Alexander whispered.

"Many things happen that cannot be explained," Ashman answered.

The stranger moved away from Ashman and glanced at me. I broke my gaze. Ashman turned around and smiled at me.

"This is Leonardo," he said, turning back to Alexander, "a little Italian boy left by his true makers in my care."

The man bowed to me. I didn't know why.

"You are my child now, Leonardo," my master whispered to me. "These creatures will look upon you the way they look upon me."

Ashman seemed a sort of master to that man as he was to me, and I felt a nagging sense of jealousy. He squeezed my hand in his and led me to another room of this place—whatever it was. There were coffins in the walls and on the floors coated with dust, and it was cold. I didn't like it. It wasn't lovely like my house.

I replayed Ashman's words in my head. *These creatures will look upon you the way they look upon me.* I couldn't help but fear what his meaning was behind those words. His movement had once again changed from almost human-like to where he looked like a phantom. *Creatures*—meaning there were…others?

"Don't be frightened, Adorato," he whispered to me. "Nobody will harm you." He brushed his hand through his hair—a very human thing to do, and it put me at ease to see it. "*Nobody* will harm you!"

I nodded.

From every corner of this vile place emerged creatures of the greatest grace and unspeakable beauty. How could *they* look upon me as anything but small, weak, and insignificant? They returned my stare, and every one of them knelt before us. Ashman squeezed tighter to my hand.

Alexander stepped forward and took my master's hand in his. He bowed slowly and kissed his hand.

"You have returned to us now," he whispered.

I heard it in his voice; he wanted to weep.

"After so many long years, you have returned, and we will forever follow you—our Cassiodorus."

Cassiodorus? At the time, I had no idea what the name meant. I cannot recall my exact feelings, but I will express them in this writing the best that I can.

I was still completely baffled by the name, and Ashman was doing little to help.

"Let me ask you," Ashman started, looking into the crowd. "How many of you came here in search of me? How many of you believed?"

I counted one by one. Six of the creatures stepped forward. Two of them were women. They looked identical except for their hair. One had hair of auburn, and the other was as black as the sky I knew. The other four were men of great beauty. Three had dark hair, the color of mine, and there was one who stood out, one whose hair had locked away the beauty of the sunlight. I stared for a long time.

"So few of you," he said.

Alexander stood.

"So few," he continued. "And the others?"

"Only followers," Alexander answered. "Creatures that are led by me."

"By you?"

"Yes." He sighed. "I believed."

"There is one whom I do not see among you, one who had always been a leader and a love of mine. Over half of you, I do not recognize. Is it so? Have all of them left the dark life?"

"Many have," Alexander replied, bowing his head in sadness. "I kept faith in you, Master. Others? As it were, others had no more to live for."

"They had Cassiodorus to live for."

He sighed.

"Where?" Ashman started, looking around for someone or something. "Where is he?"

"Who, Master?"

"The one of whom I speak, the love of mine —Cintle."

"Cintle?" Alexander cried, almost as if the name had frightened him. "My God. Master, how could you not know? Cintle is dead."

Ashman choked on his breath in shock the way a mortal would have. I saw the tears welling in his eyes. For the first time, I saw true pain and defeat in the eyes of the ancient Ashman, my master, the most powerful being I had ever encountered and probably ever will. I couldn't stand the look in his eyes, and I fell to my knees, covering my face with my hands. He looked down and knelt to meet my eyes.

"Leonardo," he whispered.

I removed my hands from my face and looked at him.

"Why on earth are you sobbing?" The pain had resided, and he was himself again.

"I'm frightened." I wrapped my arms around his neck. "I'm frightened."

He lifted me in his arms, and I felt like a little mortal boy again. He placed me in a warm bed in another nook of this—cave?

"No more tears, Leonardo," he said. "Creatures and children of mine will not weep. That is the first lesson— strength, Leonardo. You must be strong and without mortal pain, guilt, or regret. Sleep now, and when you wake, everything will be all right."

I immediately fell asleep in this catacomb, dreaming of the family I could not remember. I awoke from the feeling of warmth and saw there were torches lit around the walls. I yelled out and covered myself with the blanket from the bed, knowing full well that fire is the one thing that can really, truly hurt me.

Alexander came in and hushed me. He knew instantly what had caused me to cry out. "It will not harm you," he said. "It is used here only for light."

"But…fire—"

"Can destroy you, yes, but these torches cannot hurt you. It is only the intense, sustained heat of a fire that can cause your body to never again rise, for if there is nothing to rise—there is nothing to rise."

He ran his hand through the flame and gasped. "It is only pain, young one. You are safe, Child of Ashman."

To be known by all as the blood child of Ashman the Great—the ancient vampire from the land of sand and stone—was the most amazing feeling. Not only had I encountered a creature of such age and magnificence, but I was his child, and he loved me.

~Leonardo

The nights have passed, and I haven't touched ink to this paper in quite some time. This group of blood hunters, Ashman calls *The Children of Cassiodorus*.

William paused from his typing and thought about the truth behind the journal. For what reason, if any, would Daniel want to remember such things? There was much more to his life than imagined, so William skipped ahead to the next event in the tragic life of Daniel.

Every feed caused me pain. Every mortal I killed brought back the need for love—the need for Anya. I had to have my Anya. I was her Daniel. I *am* her Daniel.

I had to know how it came to be that I am this creature of the night. Many times, I walked near my old house, almost painfully yearning for it. I watched Anya dream but never spoke a word to her. Every night, my feet ached to carry me into my home, my hands ached to reach out to Anya, and my soul ached for answers.

Thaddeus, how could you have done this to me? Why did you create me, turn me into a monster and then leave me all alone?

I sank to my knees and covered my face with my hands. I felt warmth, so I turned to see Ashman standing there with a torch in his hand. I made the human reaction of gasping. I had never seen him more hard or emotionless since the first night I met him. I grabbed the torch from his hand, and with a scowl and a fit of brewing tears, I tossed it through the window of my old house and began going mad with fury. I screamed for Thaddeus, screamed until I cracked the windows of the burning house. I covered my head with my arms and began whimpering the names of my absent masters. I felt my body dripping wet from the sudden burst of rain. I screamed even for Eric, threw my arms up and screamed his name.

I sobbed like a child, and because I did not feel the sting of Ashman's strike, I knew he was no longer standing behind me. What I did feel was the mortal gentleness of a hand on my shoulder. I quieted my weeping and turned very slowly—to see Anya. She was smiling at me sadly and knelt down beside me.

I turned away. "You shouldn't be here."

"I know," she answered, turning my face toward her and wiping away my tears. "You told me that already." Suddenly, she gasped and stared at her fingertips, then back again at me. "Daniel—you're bleeding."

"I'm all right," I said, turning away again.

"Look at me."

I didn't want to look at her. She was too beautiful and irresistible.

"Daniel?"

I turned to look at her. The rain dripped from her black eyelashes, and her scarlet hair had been separated into dampened strands. Her white flesh shimmered from its wetness, and her silken nightdress stuck to her body, outlining her beautiful frame. She was absolutely stunning.

"Oh, Anya," I whispered. I wrapped my arms around her, savoring the warmth and delicacy of her mortality, savoring the feeling and the harmony of her heartbeat. I didn't want to let go. "You really shouldn't be here," I whispered.

"I know."

Leonardo! My name was spoken angrily within my mind. I gasped, moving away from Anya, and turned, relieved to see it was not Ashman.

"Come on now," he whispered. "It's time to come home."

I looked to Anya longingly, then back to Alexander.

He signaled me to stand. I did, and Anya mirrored my every move.

"Daniel?" Her voice trailed off like dying music.

"Come on, Leonardo."

"Daniel?"

"You shouldn't be here," I said again.

Alexander put his arm around my back and pulled me along. I looked back to see that Anya was crying.

"Daniel!" she yelled.

I looked at her, watching her confusion and her misery, wishing I could enfold her in my arms and tell her everything was going to be all right.

"Pick up your feet, boy," Alexander demanded.

"Daniel!"

"You shouldn't be here!" I yelled. My voice quieted as I began to cry. "You shouldn't be here."

I awoke to see Alexander asleep on the floor beside my bed. I wondered why he had stayed with me—probably to make sure I wouldn't try to run back to Anya. When he awoke, I watched him from beneath my eyelashes, still lying as if in sleep. I saw him wipe blood from his eyes. He folded his hands as if for a purpose of more importance than I could ever know. This then was the real Alexander, unmasked and sad.

"Please, Lord," I heard him whisper, "bring Ashman back to the light."

He was speaking to the Lord. But why? Ashman told us all that the Lord hates us, and Alexander weeps by himself when he is alone or thinks nobody can see him. Why does he cry? For what reason does he cry? Ashman told me also that no children of his will shed tears, but Alexander does, as do I. Does Ashman weep in secret when he thinks nobody knows?

I waited until Alexander turned his back to stir from my bed. He turned to look at me, and every deep emotion of pain and defeat I had seen only moments ago had given way to a sudden flood of love and gentleness.

"Leonardo," he said kindly, "you awake early."

"Do I?"

"The skies are still blue."

"Are they?"

"Yes," he said, laughing. "Don't be angry with me. I will tell Ashman nothing of Anya."

I smiled. The feeling of delicacy and grace that he entertained so masterfully almost made me believe the tears he had secretly shed in my presence had been nothing but visions from a dream.

Tears. We shed them together. Ashman cannot know. I love Alexander. He loves me too. He treats me the way I imagine my father would. Ashman tells me he loves me all the time, yet he spends the nights speaking to the others about Lucifer and the hatred of the Lord, the things that make Alexander so despaired. There was something that had diminished from their hearts.

I harkened in vain for a sense of understanding. I need to ask Ashman who these creatures are and who belongs to the name that Alexander speaks, the name —Cassiodorus.

~Leonardo Daniel

Chapter Five

"DO NOT BRING those words to the ears of Ashman," he whispered. "It will only cause him pain, Leonardo—to know you can never believe in his teachings will hurt him. He loves you, boy."

"It will cause *you* pain to keep it from him," I said. "I don't want you to cry, Alexander, not when I have the power to make things better."

"But you don't, my love," he answered, sighing. "Ashman will continue his teachings whether we approve or not."

I sighed and sank my head low.

Alexander lifted my chin and looked at me, smiling thinly. "The only way you can cause me sadness or lament, Leonardo," he whispered softly, "would be to tell me you don't love me."

I smiled. "I will always love you."

"And as long as I know that, I can share a secret with you, a painful secret, and I can speak of it without shedding a tear."

"Yes—?"

"There were some creatures here that I remember well," he started, "remember as if they are a part of me. One of them was Cintle." He took a deep breath of the mortal air, which was quite human as well as unexpected —it meant something. "Yes, Cintle was his name, a Greek come here from the island of Rhodes, sometime before Christ, as a settler of the Marseilles Harbor. He was like a leader to us, Cintle was, that is—after Ashman left us."

"Left you?"

"He was testing our faith in him," he said. "He never did tell us he was selling himself to the fire, but after so many eons of life, it made sense for us all to believe so."

"So, he was…here? This entire time?"

He shook his head. "Eze. Southern France. When he left us, he left to many places, traveled the world, Leonardo. Then he came to Italy, and he found you. I can only guess you must have been alone."

"I can't remember."

"He gave you to Thaddeus and Eric to bind them to him. He failed."

"They left."

"They did."

"I always believed Ashman had taken me because he loved me."

"Oh, but he does love you," he answered, relieving me. "He chose you for his companions not only out of his love for them but also his love for you."

I nodded. "What happened after he left you?"

"Before his departure, he told us to find the child of

Verarsoe—the evil Verarsoe Mirior. He wanted his child for our coven. His name was Relone Akar. We brought him to us when he was only very young, weak, and with so much more still left to learn. As the coven members became older and stronger, he did as well. I will not tell you about the ending of my coven, for that in itself is too painful to even think on, though I will tell you that over half of them are no longer living as followers of Ashman if they are living at all."

I thought for a moment. Relone Akar? A coven leader no older than myself? How is it possible?

"His love for the Lord." Alexander chuckled in response to my thoughts.

I smiled. "He belongs to the name Cassiodorus?"

I saw Alexander freeze for a moment. He became expressionless. He looked at me and saw my concern and instantly let the expression come back to his face and sighed.

"Cassiodorus," he whispered. Sighing again, he began. "Cassiodorus was a great leader of the Christian faith and a Venetian like you, Adorato. It was the year 480 when the man by the name of Flavius Magnus Cassiodorus was born. In his early years, he rose to an incredibly high rank in the administration of Theodoric, the ruler of Italy. In his later years, he devoted his life to religious affairs and founded a double monastery. He was a great leader to the people of Italy in his time."

"But why him?" I asked.

He chuckled. "Relone asked the same question."

"Cassiodorus was a companion of Ashman. Ashman was a great follower as well as a friend to him. But Cassiodorus, being mortal as he was, eventually died, and

Ashman continued his teachings. Now he is back leading them down a different path."

"So that's it?" I questioned. "Religion? Ashman formed a coven to teach the ways of the Lord, and now he has returned to lead them along the path to Hell? Making his loyal companionship with this wonderful man mean nothing?"

"Leonardo—"

"I will never understand him, Alex."

"I know. Nor will I. Get some sleep, Leonardo. It's getting late."

"Why did he shun me when I was sad? When I was angry? Alexander!"

He turned around, smiling.

"Please don't leave yet. I don't want to sleep alone. Please don't leave me alone."

He smiled and lay on the floor beside my bed as he had the night that I had gone to see Anya.

"Here, please," I said. "Here—beside me, please."

He looked at me strangely.

"I am sure…that I want you beside me."

He smiled again. Lord, how I love him. He slept beside me that morning, and I nestled close, wishing as I did that it were my very own father.

Alexander *is* my father now. He told me he could be my father. Of course, Ashman loves me, but he never speaks to me anymore. He remains expressionless and emotionless. He calls himself the angel of Satan. How is it that such an intense believer in the Lord's love can suddenly become—evil? Ashman's life is a secret, as I am willing to accept, but whatever it is that has caused him his loss in faith, I hope for his sake that it wasn't a lost love.

Many times, I have seen Ashman entering down another flight of stairs to a lower level of the catacomb. Each time I see him walking back up the steps, he entertains expressions of pure grief. I wanted to know what it was that was down there, what it was that caused him pain. I had even seen him wipe blood from his eyes not but three days ago. I am frightened. He is hiding something.

And so, it was as I said. I told Ashman Anya would be forever bound in my dreams, and so she is—chained to the walls of my memory. I realize she can never be made one of us, but yet I want to tell her why. I also want to tell her it is not because Ashman won't allow it but because I haven't the strength. I can't make her believe that I don't love her. I want to be the one to protect my darling Anya; I want to make sure no harm ever comes to her, that nobody but me ever touches her. I love her more than my dark life and all of the wonders it has brought me.

~Daniel

Last night, my father wouldn't let me out.

"I know what you are thinking, Leonardo, and I will not allow it. If you love me and if you love Ashman as you say you do, then you will not go to her again."

"If you love *me* as you say you do, then you will not forbid it. Please, Alexander. Please do not keep me from the one I love."

"Please, Leonardo," he begged, putting his hands on my shoulders. "Please do not defy Ashman."

"He won't hurt me," I coaxed. "Ashman loves me, even if he doesn't always remember. Please—let me go."

He sighed and turned away. "Return unharmed then, Adorato."

I put my hand on his shoulder and whispered a few words of thanks.

I left my underground home and brought myself to Anya's window. I saw she was still awake, lying in bed, tears streaming down her perfect face. My heart sank within me, but I recoiled, and I built up the courage to tap lightly on the glass. She sprang from her bed and turned to the window. Her smile warmed me even through the freeze of the night. The lament she had entertained in her expression only moments ago had completely vanished. I understood suddenly—the difference between us, not in the way that she was a woman and I was a man, but in the way that she was human and I was not. I thought coldly about my creation. I sensed the clumsiness and the rank of her doom, and I found myself almost looking at her with loathing. I am not even the same nature as a man. I don't feel temperature like a man. I don't exist on the same diet as a man—I am something more than only human.

I looked at Anya. I could smell her flesh and her sweat. I could see the life in her body. I saw the age behind her eyes and the death that awaited her. Formerly, I fancied her because she was mortal. She was beautiful to me because she was doomed, but now I looked upon her with disgust. At the same time I knew I loved her, I wanted to get away from her.

She noticed my unease. "Daniel? Are you all right?"

Her voice was like a choir to my ears, but I didn't

want to touch her. She was weak and dirty, fragile as well, and I could hurt her with my strength. She reached out to me, and I took a step back.

"Daniel, what's the matter with you? You've been acting strange."

"I shouldn't be here." But I whispered it, and she couldn't hear me with her mortal ears.

"Daniel? Will you not speak to me?"

I continued to step back, repeating to myself, *I shouldn't be here. I shouldn't be here.* I repeated it until it became nothing more than a meaningless chant. I stumbled backward and fell to the floor, covering my face with my arms as though I thought she would hurt me, as if she were Ashman standing above me with his hand raised to strike me.

Shouldn't be here, shouldn't be here, shouldn't be here. I whimpered it, rocking back and forth. I felt her stroking my dark hair, and I slowly removed my arms from my face.

She whispered sweetly to me. "What's wrong, my love?"

"I'm frightened," I whispered, loud enough for her to hear me. I knew I couldn't tell her why. "Of Ashman. I shouldn't be here. My master will punish me."

"Shh," she soothed.

My uncomfortable feelings had left me, and she was beautiful again.

"When you are older and your teachings are complete, you will be free of him. Depart to your bed before sunrise, Daniel. Don't be afraid."

I twisted a strand of her blood-red hair between my fingers as I had always loved to.

"Look at me, Daniel," she whispered, "and tell me you love me. Tell me that you can still be mine."

"I love you, Anya, and I will forever be yours."

She leaned in and kissed my temple. She whispered seductively in my ear—her words slow and soft. "Dance with me."

My heart was pounding. I was terrified of hurting her but even more terrified of Ashman finding me.

I stood to my feet, and she followed. I took her delicate hand in mine. She felt like a fragile, porcelain doll. I feared touching her with my power, but I couldn't control the spontaneous overflow of passion. I took her softly in my arms, and we danced. I ached to tell her all my secrets. I wanted to spill out everything I was, everything I knew while holding her tightly in my arms. The dance was only a reason to be close. There was almost no movement in our feet; I didn't want to do anything but hold her.

We halted, and I embraced her then. I could hear the blood rushing through her veins. I could smell it—taste it. I wanted it. I kissed her neck, and she didn't stop me. I controlled the urge to plunge my teeth into her neck and moved away.

"Don't stop," she whispered.

I nibbled gently, not intending on hurting her. She breathed a few lovely words, but I wasn't listening; all I could hear was the river of her blood. I opened my mouth before I could stop myself, and I bit.

She gasped and pulled away, screaming at the sight of blood on my teeth. I tried to hush her. Her screams were miserable sounds. I covered her mouth and grasped her throat to quiet her.

Seconds later, she lay there—dead at my feet.

I wept in his arms that morning. I was a monster now. I destroyed the only purity and innocence I will ever know.

"Perhaps not dead," I whispered. "Perhaps not dead but in sleep."

"You cannot return, Adorato. Please listen to me." He moved away from our embrace and put his hands on my shoulders.

I watched the human wrinkles in his forehead move while he looked closely at me. I moved my gaze to his black eyes.

"It is not our place to converse with mortals," he said. "Ashman is right—we must hide in the shadows and remain in the shadows."

I sighed and bowed my head. "I know. I tried to be someone else, and I failed. All I wanted to do was love her—and now I have destroyed her."

"It is not evil that consumes you, my darling. It is grief. You are more human than any immortal I have met. Do not wash away your lingering humanity just to no longer feel. What I wouldn't give to feel what you are feeling now, Leonardo."

"What do you mean?"

"I wish that for once I could be consumed by the human pain that has befallen you. I wish for once I could feel alive again, that I could feel…human."

I sighed. "I love you, Father."

He embraced me again. "I know."

~Daniel

. . .

It was last night when I discovered my master's secret. I watched him once more walking up the steps from that lower floor, wiping blood from his eyes. I gasped and backed deeper into the darkness of the room. I am sure he sensed me, but for some reason, he remained silent, as if he wanted me to know what it was that he was keeping from us. I waited until I knew he wouldn't see me and crept slowly down the steps. It was difficult to see, even with my gifted eyes—it was nearly impossible. I let my eyes slowly adjust and gazed around the room. I gasped and stared in awe. Everywhere around me...stood Ashman's white stoned statues.

His power was beyond anything I ever dreamed of. In the exact same places, still completely flawless, not a single one was missing. I stepped closer to the figure of the beautiful Egyptian woman, the one Ashman had said he would never speak a word of—and alas, he hadn't. I touched the face of the statue, studying her beauty with my hands. I was dumbstruck.

Who was she? Who was she to Ashman? My master remains a mystery to me still. Alas, his grief was caused by the loss of a love—the one thing I hoped for his sake was not the cause for his misery. It made me think of Anya.

"I am cursed," I whispered to myself.

Just then, the face of that woman lit up, a beautiful orange light illuminating her features. I smiled and reached out to touch the perfectly sculpted face.

"LEONARDO!"

I gasped, almost falling over. I turned to see my father with a torch in his hand.

"Are you mad?"

"I just wanted to see."

He grasped my cloak and pushed me forward.

"Out, Leonardo—now!"

I raced up the steps as fast as I could and concealed myself in my bedroom. Alexander followed.

"You should know better," he said calmly.

"Oh, I do, Father," I insisted, "but I just couldn't bear not knowing what it was that he was hiding down there."

"Her name was Lanara," he said softly.

"What? She was… You…*knew* her."

He sighed heavily. "She was Ashman's ancient love, Adorato. She died many centuries ago. The truth is true love—never dies."

"He is in agony."

He nodded. "He is."

"I had no idea. Why didn't you tell me?"

"Because it was not your place to know, Leonardo. That's why."

"Forgive me, Father," I whispered. "I only wanted to know."

"I understand. You will learn in time."

"I fear I will never learn—not as long as I stay here."

He sighed. "Get some sleep, Leonardo. It's for the best."

~Daniel

Chapter Six

ALEXANDER CAME in to wake me not but four days ago. It has been five days since my last entry, and I have now finally stopped weeping over Anya, though I still dream of her every night.

When I awoke that evening, I saw that my father was smiling. His revealed fangs enchanted me. I reached out to touch them and gasped as one of them pricked my fingertip. Alexander moved my finger to his lips and took the blood away.

"Sweet like your youth," he told me. "Innocent like your love."

I smiled.

"Come now, Leonardo. I'll take you out to hunt again."

"I dreamed of her again," I said, sliding off my bed. "In my dream, I was dancing with her, and when she kissed me, I could feel her…fangs...against my lip."

"It was only a dream, Adorato."

"Yes, but aren't dreams in some ways visions? Mirrors of the future?"

"No more, Leonardo," he whispered. "It was only a dream."

"I would like to believe that somehow Anya is alive, that somehow she still loves me."

"Leonardo, you must let her go," he cried. "Please, boy, for the love of God, forget her. Just live as though you never knew her."

"She is forever bound to me, Father. What you ask of me is impossible."

He sighed. "Then keep quiet about her. It only makes things worse."

I nodded.

My father took me out to hunt that night. I had enjoyed the taste of the old beggar I took and the man whose throat I opened while he slept. I would like to think they are in Heaven (if such a place exists). My father and I prayed for them—prayed to the God Ashman claims does not exist. I wonder how many others that belong to Ashman's coven cry or pray when they are alone.

I miss Ashman these days. He never speaks to me anymore. He spends all his time alone or leading the others down the path to Hell. I don't wish to stay here any longer. I stay for Alexander; I stay because I have nowhere else to go. I need to grow and to change. I don't feel alive here in this place; there is just too much wrong with it. I feel dead. Ashman says we are all dead and that is why we cannot die. Alexander says differently.

"We are not dead, Leonardo." He chuckled. "But neither are we alive. We are something in between that nobody has created a logical word for. Mortals would call us the undead. I say we are alive, Leonardo. I would say we are alive because we feel. We feel fear, happiness, sorrow, pain. We feel as mortals feel. We feel like the living, do we not?"

I smiled, and he laughed quietly.

"You are more human than monster. That is what Relone always told us. We have human bodies, human blood—and human hearts too." He was smiling. "I know your thoughts," he started, his smile instantly transforming to utter worry. "I can read you, Adorato."

I stared at him hard—desperately.

"Ah, Adorato," he whispered. "I love you, boy, but there is somewhere you can go that will not cause you pain."

"You wish for me to leave, Father?"

"Of course not, but I would never do anything to cause you pain, and me keeping you here would be selfish—that would hurt you."

"I love you, Father, but there is something wrong with this place."

"Oh, Leonardo, there is everything wrong with it. It is dull. It is frightening. It is dark and lifeless. This is a cage —not a home."

"So, you see it too?"

He nodded. "I would go with you, but I cannot. I cannot live outside these walls, Leonardo. I have spent too many centuries here—underground."

I sighed. "Ashman…he will never let me go."

"He will. He sees now the time has come for you to leave him."

"I need to discover who—or *what* I am. I need to

change and to grow older and stronger, and then—I can return."

"You will never return."

"I will."

"You will never return here, Leonardo." He turned away.

"Why do you say this?"

"Because I know it," he answered solemnly. "Once you leave this place, it will never again feel right spending even a moment here."

I touched his shoulder. "Where is this place, Alexander?"

He turned toward me. He was in agony, but there were no tears. "Before I let you leave—make me a promise."

"A promise?"

He nodded. "A promise…in blood. Promise me you will return to me someday, Adorato. Promise you will return for one final farewell."

"You know I will."

"Again—you needn't tell Ashman you are leaving."

I nodded. "Where is it?" I asked again. "This place, Alexander."

"Secret," he answered. "Tell no one else."

"I swear it."

Alexander handed me a golden chalice with a good gill of his blood in it. I was to add some of mine as well. We both drank from it to seal my pact of return. The blood was sweet, and I could feel the strength of my father running through my veins. I sat beside him for long moments before I could speak.

"Alexander," I started quietly, "where do I go?"

"Far away, through the woods."

"The woods?"

"Through the woods. You will find a graveyard. If you sit upon the ground and wait—he will find you."

"Who? Alexander—who will find me?"

"Leonardo, I am sending you to somebody who can care for you."

I nodded.

"I don't want you to be afraid," he continued. "I know him well. He is old and strong, and if you mention my name, he will not be able to turn you away."

"Will you not tell me his name?"

"His name…" He paused and leaned toward me, whispering in my ear, "Cintle."

When Alexander first spoke the name, the pain I had seen in Ashman's eyes that had made me cry flashed in my mind and replayed continuously.

"The auburn-haired companion of Ashman," I choked. It was hard to speak.

He nodded. He was sad.

"You told Ashman he was dead," I cried. "You did. I was there. You said he was dead. Why? Why would you say something that would cause Ashman so much agony, Alexander? I don't understand."

"I don't expect you to understand. Cintle is dead. He is dead to Ashman. Cintle will never return here. Because of his love for me, he let me know he was alive. He let me know where he was going. I was sworn to secrecy. I had to let the others believe in his death."

"Why?"

"Cintle promised us—the others and me—that he

would lead us alongside Relone, that he would be here until his death. He made a pact."

"Loyalty."

"Yes. If the others knew he left, some would go after him, intending on destroying him for his lies. Others would fall into great sorrow. He has gone to live the way he chooses to live. The same reason you are leaving—to change. He has never returned. It's forbidden to leave a coven. I never had another chance to tell him I loved him."

"Please don't cry, Alexander."

He turned back to face me. "I refuse. Do this, Leonardo. Find Cintle and keep him as your master. He lives in the world of light—the way you dream of living. I can see it in your soul that he is good for you."

"I *will* see you again," I said.

"Tell him I love him?"

"I shall. I promise."

Our parting was long and warm. We stayed together through the day, and by nightfall, I was tired but on my way.

The night was cold, and I had very little comfort. I miss Alexander already and Ashman too. I tucked the chalice into my satchel. It is the only thing I have to remind me of home. The only thing besides these words. I am in the graveyard right now, the one that Alexander had told me to find. I will stop writing for now. May my next entry be enjoyable to write.

~Daniel

. . .

And so it is. I'm writing this with a smile on my face. At this moment, I am very warm but very lonely. Two nights ago, as I sat in that graveyard, I felt a great tremble beneath me and the loud sound of a heartbeat. I jumped from the ground, grasping my journal close to my chest. I leaned against a tree to keep my balance. The soil where I had been sitting began to stir and writhe, and from the dirt rose two white hands and a lovely sight of soiled, auburn hair. I gasped, which was a very human thing to do, and closed my eyes for a moment. When at last the creature had completely risen and shaken the dirt from his body, he turned and locked his eyes on me. He made me nervous, and I was trembling. He approached me. He didn't look angry. He was completely expressionless, as Ashman usually was.

"Who are you?" he growled. His voice sounded… almost human, and I relaxed a little.

I tried to speak, but I was breathless. I was able to choke out one word. "Alexander."

The creature took a step back and froze, the way a mortal would have, and his face now held more emotion than I had ever seen in Ashman or even my Alexander when he was sobbing. He squinted his eyes and recoiled in curiosity. He stepped closer to me again, and I could feel his breath on my neck—the way I had Eric's the last night I had been alive. He bit through the flesh of my neck, and I let out a long gasp. I wasn't sure if it was from discomfort or pain. He pulled back after scarcely taking blood.

"Alexander…" he whispered. "You are his child."

I shook my head.

"You drank from him."

I nodded.

"How? How can it be?" He sounded hurt. I was still only hardly breathing, so it was hard for me to speak.

"Ashman," I whispered. It was so quiet I wasn't sure at first if he had even heard me.

"Ashman!" He cried. His voice lowered to a whisper, and he bowed his head. "He was right."

He began speaking to himself. I heard several mumbles and whispers, but I couldn't tell what he was saying. I knew he had said something about Ashman's return and verbalized apologies for many people whose names I did not recognize, but some I did—such as Alexander. He was pacing, mumbling nonsensical phrases. He halted in front of me, and it startled me.

"Why are you here?"

"For you," I answered. "I need to grow and to change, and as long as I remained there, I couldn't. Alexander told me the secret of your leaving the old coven led by Relone Akar. I swore I would not tell another—I will not tell another!"

"Who are you?"

"Le—" I stopped, bowed my head, and whispered, "Daniel."

"Daniel?"

"My name is Daniel."

He nodded and moved his fingers to his lips, which was very humanlike. "How has my Alexander changed?"

"I cannot say," I answered. "Still a lover of the Lord —strong."

"And Ashman?"

"Ashman is not himself. Alexander explained to me the way he used to be, the leader of a religious coven. He is leading the 'new' members down the path to Hell. He said the Lord hates us and our true leader is Lucifer."

"Lucifer?" he cried. "But Relone—Cassiodorus!"

"I have heard every word of them both from Alexander," I answered. "May I ask you a question?"

He looked at me.

"Why am I not frightened of you? Why do you seem as young as me?"

He laughed quietly, and I found it very charming. "I am a believer in the Lord," he said. "I have a lot of humanity left within me—for reasons, Daniel. I have held on to my humanity. I have prayed for my victims and asked forgiveness from the Lord. God does not hate us, Daniel. Truly he doesn't. We are what we have been made into, whatever it may be. We live the way we are forced to live. We cannot change what we are, my young friend, and the Lord does not condemn us for that."

"So, the Lord—he is—*our* Lord?"

"Yes," he answered. "The devil promises nothing, Daniel. You know this."

"I do. Alexander told me."

He smiled, but it faded. "So, my Ashman has turned from the light?"

"He has."

"It's as I've always feared," he whispered. "Cassiodorus has lost his faith."

"Whatever happened to your former leader?"

"Relone?"

I nodded.

He smiled. "The coven ended. After I left, there was nothing. I wonder if he is still here or if he is alone or not.

Whatever happened to Relone, I do not know. There was never much of a farewell between us."

I looked at him sadly and bowed my head.

"Don't be hurt for me," he said, smiling, lifting my chin to look into his eyes. I watched the human wrinkles in his forehead disappear as his eyebrows lowered. "Tell me why you need me."

"You're very kind," I told him.

He smiled. "Go on. Tell me."

"I need a leader, a master. Somebody who can lead me as I change and grow stronger."

He smiled and nodded. "I can do that. For Alex."

He was so kind to me that I wanted to embrace him. I wanted to be close to him.

"Don't worry," he said. "There was no need to invade your mind to know you need this."

He embraced me the way Alexander would have. He was so different than I had expected; he was so tender, kind, and warm. I could feel while in his arms that he was strong. I felt age. He was beautiful.

"I will keep you," he said.

I smiled, moving away from him.

"Forgive me." He chuckled. "You aren't difficult to read."

"As I have learned," I answered. "There was never a word in my mind that was ever only my own while I was with Alexander."

Cintle hunted with me that night, and because of his placidness and his kindness, I already felt a closeness to him, almost an intimacy. That night just before sunrise, he told me I would have to sleep in the ground.

"The ground?" I asked him, thinking I had misunderstood.

He nodded. "To hide from the sun. Don't be afraid. I've been doing it this way for two centuries."

That evening, we dug our graves and went to sleep. I don't like the ground; it's cold, and the dirt sticks in my hair and in my mouth. I don't like feeling alone either. I can't feel Cintle beside me, and I hate it. I miss Alexander and Ashman, I miss Anya, and I weep for them. I cried just hours ago, and Cintle was there to comfort me.

"I'm sick to death of being sad," I told him. "Sick to death of caring so much about everything. I don't want to care anymore, Master—about anything. I don't want to feel any more hurt."

He looked at me sadly, wiping moisture from his own eyes, and whispered, "Neither do I."

I sat there, thinking about Anya and the family that I couldn't remember. I think I had a sister, a pretty one. I wish I could see her now. Cintle told me that perhaps if I tell myself long enough that I don't care, I might just stop feeling altogether. I pretend I don't care about Anya. After all, why should I? She was mortal, meaning weak and dirty—nothing to me. Of course, if this were true, I wouldn't keep the name Daniel. The name is a constant reminder that I once loved her; it has now been transformed into a constant reminder to be strong.

Even within these words—my writings will begin as

less than the truth about how I feel, but I hope that will soon change to the point where I no longer have to lie to myself to be strong.

I need to realize I am no longer a mortal child—I am no longer a child at all, and so I tell myself that I do not mind sleeping in the ground, and I do not need the comfort of company. I don't care. I *can't* care!

William read the words, and as he did, he wanted to cry, not for Daniel's pain but for the passion he felt and the sadness that consumed him when he read the lies of which Daniel had written.

He read furiously for the next few days, learning of the love that Daniel shared with Cintle, just as he did with Alexander. The sweet innocent Daniel had become a cold, regretless killer.

As the pages turned, the years passed, and Daniel wrote less and less. The next event in his life was distressing and heartbreaking, but the only one who wept was William.

Cintle told me about God. He told me there is no other above him, and there is nothing that can be done to make God stop loving us. The Lord loves unconditionally, and whether we are blood hunters or human, doomed, or immortal, God loves us; he forgives us for our sins.

"So, the flames of Hell do not await us after death?"

He shook his head. "If death ever does come, only the white shores of Heaven await."

I tried not to smile. I tried not to be relieved. I wasn't

afraid of Hell. I am *not* afraid of Hell—I am not afraid of anything.

Cintle told me he could feel my strength increasing, and it brought up my spirits, but I realized when he said it, there was a tone of remorse in his voice.

Immediately following our conversation about God, Cintle led me into the woods; there, he showed me a large circle of cleared land where he had piled branches and sticks in the center of the clearing.

He put his hands on my shoulders. "No tears, Daniel."

I closed my eyes at his touch, my name said in his voice reminding me to be strong.

"I can never be like you," he said sadly. "I can never feel no pain or regret. I've spent too much of my life feeling pain. I cannot live with myself, and I cannot let my weakness bring you down. I love you, Daniel—you know that."

"I do, Master, but—what are you telling me?"

He lifted his hands and smiled before he plunged them down with an angry fit brewing in his eyes. I jumped back with a yell, feeling quite foolish by my reaction. Cintle had set a fire with the power of his mind, the same way Ashman had.

"Master—Cintle—what are you telling me?"

"That my time has come, Daniel."

"What?"

"The fire, my love."

"Master, fire is the one thing that can…destroy us."

"Exactly."

"What? You can't mean—you can't throw yourself into the fire!"

"Of course I can!" he answered. "No fear, no pain."

I stepped farther back and turned away as Cintle jumped into the red flames. His gorgeous smile faded, and his white skin became charred and fell to ashes. I wouldn't cry. I don't care—right? I can't change any more. I have tried and failed. Cruelty takes the place of my tears. I wear a mask of strength. On the inside, I cry. On the inside, I scream, I bawl—I am weak.

I stared at the flames and caught a glimpse of a quavering face watching with anguish at the ashes of my beloved master. I could see he was no older than myself when he was made. He was beautiful with deep, tense brown eyes and hair the color of the smoke that rose from Cintle's pyre.

"Wait!" I called. "Please—"

But he was gone.

He had been weeping over Cintle's death. Can't I weep too? Who was he? Who was this weak immortal come too late for my master? I want to grieve. I will not lie, not in these writings. On the inside, I am weak. I sat in front of that fire until the flames died, and still, as the wood of my master's pyre ceased to burn, I sat there solemnly until the sun began to rise. I slept in the ground and dreamed of my loves—Anya, Cintle, Alexander, Ashman, and blood. I was hungry again.

~Daniel

I know it has actually been months since I have last written, and there is a lot to write. I will shorten it the best that I can. I had been walking for hours a night for the past few months without much rest and without much blood either. I don't know where I am, but I discovered that the speed I possessed was a lot stronger than I had ever realized. I knew I was no longer even in Russia; I had traveled around the world without even realizing the change in my surroundings. My sorrow is all I am consumed by—my grief. There is no comfort for me. I don't know where I am. My mind has been poisoned by my mourning and has been so clouded that the trek from Russia had seemed like nothing more than a nightly search for warm, fresh blood.

It was a few nights ago when I was pushing the thoughts of my family aside that I found a family, an evil one—father and son, planning a murder for money. I was hungry to the point of pain, and I saw my chance.

Suddenly disrupting my plans came a thought—I would seek out the rival family they were after, just to see. I invaded their minds. My curiosity drove me to something I never imagined.

Find them I did—with ease. What I found was a miserable boy named Victor Miller, who loved nothing more than his mother. A beautiful boy with hair that brought the sunlight back into my life, his eyes shades of amber even in the darkness. He was a poor boy with a love for poetry and a great passion for acting. This family I had watched deserved nothing but love, especially the eldest son—he didn't quite fit in. He isn't right in his world. While his father and brothers labor in the fields under the hot sun (which I do not miss very much), he is inside reciting poetry to his mother's charming piano music. As I watched him, I came to realize that although he loves his family, he would have been rid of his father and brothers if he could. I don't want their enemies to kill them. All they want is his father's land.

I realize that Victor will hate me if I take him away from his family (especially his lovely porcelain doll of a mother), so I have decided to let the Millers' wicked enemies fulfill their plans, but I will rescue Victor and give him revenge against the Cornallys.

~Daniel

It has been about a week since last I wrote, and the time is getting closer to the Millers' death. I should not involve myself with affairs of the living; I should leave and never again think on what may happen to them. I don't care, do I? I sigh as I write this because as I watch Victor, I see in him a vibrant light. He is so full of passion; all he needs is the opportunity to express it. I will not lie. I care about Victor, and I want to care about him. I want to save him.

~Daniel

Right now, as I write, my beautiful Victor lies asleep in the room above the one in which I sit. His blood gave to me all of his secrets, and I know him now. I am afraid for myself. I have loved so many and lost them all. What will become of me when I lose Victor as well? I return to Victor tonight after a short absence. The time for his revenge is nearing.

I am writing what I believe to be the beginning of the end of this journal. I must just write that my darling Victor will fulfill the murder of the Cornallys. Now, as I have Victor, as I hope I always will, there seems no need to write anymore. What good will it do anybody? There is something about him, by his eyes, that makes it impossible to forget him or any word spoken by him. My biggest fear is to forget. Victor is all I want to remember, and when I look into his eyes, he washes over me a flood of memories. With Victor, I will never forget.

And so, I *have made* mistakes, as strong as it may be. It started with the night I destroyed the Foster family. I clearly remember it when I look at Victor because I did it for him.

I saw a lovely little auburn-haired child asleep in a bed. I saw an opportunity to do something for Victor. I should have taken the Cornallys. I should have simply killed them and let the Millers go on living. My rescuing Victor was more selfish than anything else I could have done, and all I wanted to do was make things better. I fear deeply that one day, my beloved child will find out what I did to his family. I stared at the tiny little child, but before I had time to bring myself to her, I was disturbed by an unfamiliar presence.

"For whom?" I heard.

I spun around and sighed. "For Victor. I want her because…I love Victor."

"Or you want her because you fear he will leave you?"

I sighed. "Please. Why are you speaking to me? Who are you?"

He chuckled. "That doesn't matter. To bring a mortal child home to bind your immortal child to you is a sin. It is forbidden, Daniel!"

"Leave me!" I demanded with a wave of my hand.

"You will regret this, my young friend, if you do this."

I sighed again. *It is because I love him,* I thought.

"I love him as well as you do."

"What? What are you talking about? And stop reading my thoughts!"

"I know him as well as you," he said. "I have been watching him with my immortal eyes longer than you, and I love him too. If he finds out what you have done—if you do it—he will despise you forever."

"You cannot tell him!" I demanded, stepping toward him.

He stared motionless, his brown eyes full of so much strength. His hair was a mass of black curls.

"Please! You cannot tell him. I am doing this because I love him."

"Victor knows you are out to take the Fosters tonight," he said. "He knows."

"But he cannot know that this child is Anna Foster!" I yelled. "I have been watching the Fosters for weeks, that he knows, but he can never know that I destroyed her family and left her alone. He would never forgive me. I already let his family die as I shouldn't have, and this, I am doing to make up for it." I broke my gaze from the house back to his face. "Why have you concerned yourself with me? Who are you?" I waited for his voice again with that gentle French accent.

"Allow me to introduce myself," the vampire started, bowing formally. "King Verarsoe Mirior."

The King? What could the king have wanted with me? The taking of Anna was forbidden, but I have committed the crime, and I am still here. Perhaps if Victor truly knew me—he would hate me.

~Daniel

. . .

William wanted the answers, the truth about what happened between Victor and his maker, but as he read, he wasn't given what he wanted to know. The years passed, and Anna had been made a vampire by Daniel's blood and shared a deep love with Victor. Daniel was sickened by the thoughts of what he had done to her. He feared that one day, the truth would be revealed. His guilt consumed him. He could not look at Victor or Anna without pain and guilt, so he gathered his things, and he left to France. He later came to the underground mansion of the king, and there he found Victor, but not Anna. Victor's hate for Daniel when Verarsoe revealed the truth to him caused a bitter parting between them. William wept.

Chapter Seven

"I'M RETURNING it to you anyway," he answered, extending his hand without raising his head. He smiled.

"Are you certain you don't want to keep it?" Daniel asked. "Because you can if you desire it."

He shook his head. "I want you to have it."

"You can look at me," the vampire said. "Don't be afraid of me."

William slowly raised his head.

The vampire smiled and took his journal from William's hand.

"What happened?" he asked.

"Happened?"

"Later, after the journal, after you stopped writing."

He laughed, and William jumped back.

"Don't be so terrified of me," Daniel declared. "I do not wish to harm you. Even in a time of weakness, I couldn't harm you. You remind me too much of Victor."

He smiled.

"I can tell you," Daniel said, "if you truly wish to

know."

"I do."

"After Victor found out what had happened and decided to let himself hate me, I realized I had to find another, lest my loneliness would drive me to madness. The guilt of what I had done to Victor, letting the Cornallys destroy his family and then letting Verarsoe destroy little Anna's family as well, everything I had done, it would be nearly impossible to bring myself to create another. I didn't create another, of course, but I did meet a girl on the streets.

"She was on an evening walk when I found her. The air was moist from the day's rain. I wasn't hungry, and I am glad because she was very lovely—a head full of black ringlet curls and eyes of blue. She was so pleasing to look at. I told her what I was, and she laughed at me, but as time passed and we became close companions, she once found the courage within herself to ask me how I had such amazing abilities. She asked me how I had such speed and strength, how I could read her thoughts, and why my tears were blood when I lamented over my past. She was stunned at first, and I wasn't sure if she believed me. I still am not sure exactly when she accepted the fact that I had been telling her the truth from the very beginning. I was never sure what it was about her that made me feel like I had to always be close to her, always look after her. It was different than it was with Anya, but yet I was sure I loved her as I loved Anya.

"I remember finding her at a party one evening. She looked radiant in a blood-red gown that reached the base of her feet. She looked like an angel as she danced in the ballroom of her mansion and laughed. I wanted her then!

I can't begin to describe how perfectly beautiful she was to me. The music stopped, and she saw me standing in the doorway. She ran to me and wrapped her arms around my neck. I laughed and returned her embrace.

"'You look beautiful,' I whispered to her.

"'You always say that.' She giggled. 'I have something for you. Earlier this evening, I was out again, and a hooded woman approached me. I don't know who she was, but it was so strange. She was covered with dirt, but I do not think she was a beggar. She gave me a letter.'

"'What sort of letter?' I asked. 'What did it say?'

"'I don't know,' she answered. 'She told me to give it to you.'

"'To me?'

"'Yes. She said to me that you must have it. I'll go get it for you. Wait here.'

"I was puzzled by the way she acted. She seemed frantic, like something was terribly wrong. My curiosity was almost maddening. A letter? Who would be sending me a letter, and why?

"I waited for her, guessing she was having difficulty finding it. My curiosity grew to a terrible irritation, and I walked very slowly up the winding staircase—the grand staircase, as one might call it. I found her bedroom and knocked gently on the door, trying not to startle her.

"'Rayne?' I called. 'Rayne, are you in there, darling?'

"No answer.

"'Rayne?' I knocked again. I stood at the door, sighing, begging my mind to tell me what the mystery letter could be.

"She didn't come out. I heard a voice, a deep voice. I knew then that she wasn't alone, and I felt betrayed! It was as if she had taken my love and given me back nothing. I thought about our almost romance and wondered why I had been so foolish, why I had never just told her I loved her. It was because of the creature that I was that I couldn't let myself keep getting attached to people. It's in my nature. I love too much.

"Suddenly, I felt in my stomach a feeling of dread. Something terrible had happened, and I brought myself to break the door from its hinges. A flood of memories came sweeping over me, bringing me to my knees in tears. I could feel Victor, his presence, his life. I could smell his blood, but I could not decide why. I knew where he was —our blood had bound us—and I knew he was nowhere near here. Still, I could feel him as though he stood beside me, feel his power and his cursed life. Why?

"Rayne was nowhere to be found, and the lovely rug was drenched in blood. For a moment, I was horrified. I looked with loathsomeness at the blood on the floor and the tiny speck of tattered flesh on the edge of the dresser that I didn't need gifted eyes to see. I wept then but stopped almost instantly when I remembered the letter. Rayne wasn't dead, and I knew that. Despite the liters of blood on the floor—it was for that very reason I knew she was not dead. She was nowhere to be found, and my senses gave me the sharp feeling of a new life entering the dark world.

Who it was that had done it was the only thing I wanted to know. Who? Rayne was an equal to me now by somebody who shared Victor's blood, by either a close companion or a child of his. And now I feared that I would never see her again. She would be bound to her new master now—she loved me once."

Daniel sank his head low for a moment, lost in his thoughts.

"And the letter," he continued, "the letter was something I was not surprised to receive. I cannot understand to this day why it didn't occur to me as soon as Rayne mentioned it. I should have known.

"I opened the envelope slowly, enjoying the sound of the tearing paper. I unfolded the paper inside, and my eyes welled with tears. It read,

"Leonardo,

The years I am certain have passed like seconds to you, but not for myself. I am in agony without you. In agony without one last embrace to last me forevermore. Return to me, Leonardo. I beg of you. Return to me as you so vowed to do on your immortal blood.

All my love and compassion to you, my darling. Your loving father,

~Alexander

"I wiped the blood from my eyes, being reminded once again to be strong. Alexander had called for me, my beloved father. And of course, Ashman, the people I considered my family, who I haven't seen in over two hundred years. It was the year 1796, and Alexander had waited too long for me already. He had an address written out for me, and he was here—not in Russia where he had been when I left him. He was here—in Boston.

"Of course, I did come back to Alexander, and the underground mansion was identical to the one in Russia. I remembered everything. Even the smallest of things shot that dreamy sensation of the past through me. I froze as my father approached me. His face was so beautiful. He looked more the way I remembered him than I ever expected him to. I choked on my breath, on my tears. He did too. I could hardly move, but I was able to wrap my arms around him and let myself fall gently against him. I wept softly.

"This time, it was all right to weep.

"I felt a presence behind me. I loosened my grip around my father's back and fell passionately into the arms of my master.

"'Ashman, my master, my father, my beloved.'

"He laughed quietly. 'You came back,' he whispered.

"I smiled and looked up at him. While I was in their arms, I didn't notice the coven members surrounding us or the hooded woman who watched me. I stared back at her. She must have been the one to have given Rayne the letter. She was covered and caked with mud. Her pale skin was browned from the soil. She kept her hood on and her head bowed. She looked as though she had been asleep for decades. I believe she had. I remember the image as clearly as my very eyes see the night sky—her mud-covered hood shadowing her pale face and almost completely hidden red locks of hair. She looked up for a moment but immediately averted her eyes when she noticed I was staring at her. She bowed her head once more. I lifted her chin, guiding her to look at me, and I almost leaned in to kiss her, but I didn't. I am unsure why I didn't do what I wanted, and to this day, I do not know why I didn't open my arms and cry out, *Anya!*

"The only thing I can tell you is that it was just too late for us. My Anya remains with me only in my memories and within these words." He clutched the journal to his chest. "All of my love, my soul, my passion lives now within my red-haired maiden's sweet eyes of blue."

Chapter Eight

IT HAD BEEN two years since I finished the story of my life in those words to William, but it doesn't quite end there. Not very long ago, I sat in that room that poured evil out of every corner. I sat on the old, tattered bed, staring at the floor and crying bitterly over the memories of Anna. I move from hotel to hotel, graveyard to graveyard; I am Daniel, the loner, but something happened that night that I would never have expected.

"No more tears?" I heard.

I slowly removed my hands from my face and turned to see him standing there. He looked very human, leaning against the wall with his arms crossed in front of his chest.

He laughed. "No more tears, you said?"

I choked out a whisper as I stood to my feet. "Alex?"

He laughed and lifted his shoulders with open arms.

"You say it like you're unsure." He chuckled.

"Alex!" I stumbled into his arms, gripping his white shirt with my fingernails.

"My Leonardo," he said. "Mi adorato."

I hadn't realized he was speaking in Italian. I normally thought in Italian or Russian, but I was thinking in English.

"Oh God!" I whispered. "Alexander—Father!"

He was quietly laughing to himself.

"I thought you said you could never leave the catacomb," I said, drying my eyes with the back of my hand.

"Yes, Leonardo," he answered. "Of course I said that. I also told the entire coven—save for you—that Cintle was dead."

I smiled. "Yes, I suppose you did," I whispered, leaning back into his embrace.

"I know, but—no more tears, my love."

My Alexander had come back to me, and now centuries later in the year 1993, I continue my life as Daniel Sarcova, child of Ashman the Great and Alexander, the Russian beauty.

I wanted more. After all I had been given and all I had been through in my life—I wanted more. I wanted to know whom it was that I had seen behind the smoke of Cintle's pyre that night when I was still very young. I know now by the books of my kind, the stories by Adam —that the creature was none other than ancient Relone Akar, but I wanted to hear it from him. I wanted to find him and ask him about the ending of his coven, the ending of Cintle. Of course, Victor being my child, it wasn't difficult to find Relone. He and Victor once shared in a love that was not expected. But I tell you now—as easy as it was to find Relone, it wasn't easy to get his story from him.

"I already told my story to Victor," he said. "I needn't relive the pain again."

I apologized, of course, but was still completely unsatisfied. Perhaps begging Relone was selfish—though that has never really stopped me before, and well, you all love the selfish Adam Gold, am I right? I am unsure if we will ever hear the words from Relone about the death of my master—my beloved Cintle, my auburn-haired companion. Perhaps it is better left untold. Perhaps it would be easier for me to forget him entirely anyway.

So, I end now. In the modern era, which has now unexpectedly sprung up around us from the lovely Adam Gold, I am simply Daniel—an immortal, no bigger than that. I still live in the light—in a modern house with a blazing hearth and a beautiful chalice on the mantelpiece.

As we all crave to be famous—or infamous like the legendary Adam Gold—I have reached out to the mortal world as he has, and now, I end as he has. Farewell now, and before you call out to *me,* ask yourself—do you deserve it?

-Daniel Sarcova 1993

About the Author

Sara J Bernhardt is an author and poet who has been writing since a very young age and is a winner of several poetry and short story contests. It is clear that Bernhardt writes in a realistic tone while still creating the enthralling feeling of fantasy. Her writing puts readers in a world that they will truly love to be a part of. Though the writing is edgy and catching it is also not too complex which makes it a comfortable and enjoyable read for everyone.

You can follow Sara at these locations:

Facebook:
www.facebook.com/Sara-J-Bernhardt
Website
www.sjbernhardt.com

Other Works by Sara J. Bernhardt

Summer's Deceit (Hunters Trilogy – Book 1): Jane Callahan is a reclusive, seventeen-year-old high school student dealing with the death of her beloved brother. Her home in Southern California with her mother is a constant reminder of her loss and pain. In hopes of escaping her past she moves to North Bend Oregon to live with her father, where she meets a beautiful boy named Aidan Summers. Jane is intrigued by his looks as well as his unusual ways of attempting to get her attention. After months of uncommon conversation and frustration, an uncertain romance brews between Jane and Aidan, but Aidan has a ghastly secret that could destroy everything.

https://books2read.com/SummersDeceit

Summer's Shadow (Hunters Trilogy – Book 2): Aidan Summers, a seventeen-year-old, stunningly beautiful genius, somehow finds his way into the life of Jane Callahan; a lovely girl trapped in soggy North Bend, Oregon.

In this new Tale by Sara J. Bernhardt, Aidan relates his side of the story. All of his dark secrets are revealed and all of his motivations behind his strange ways become known as the story unravels in a captivating narrative of suspense, romance, courage...and murder.

https://books2read.com/SummersShadow

Summer's Redemption (Hunters Trilogy – Book 3): The secret alliance of The Silver Wing and the waging war with their evil rival, The Sevren, come into full view in a new light. The evil that still lurks and stirs behind the supposed destruction of The Sevren steps out of the shadows and spins a new tale of adventure, suspense, romance, mystery and terror.

https://books2read.com/SummersRedemption

Behind Blue Eyes Series

A father's desire to save his child presents him with an unthinkable choice that leaves him darker than human, forced to roam through time alone as he searches for the place he belongs.

Adam Gold – Book 1: Fleeing the French invasion of Geneva Switzerland in the 1700s, Adam Gold books passage to America with his family. On the ship, Adam's daughter falls fatally ill. A mysterious man comes to Adam with a way to save his child by turning Adam into something darker than human.

https://books2read.com/AdamGold

The Medallion – Book 2: Adam Gold, an immortal with sweet eyes of blue, rushes through the centuries on a quest for reason and a thirst for revenge. To cope with his pain and regret, he sleeps away the years and awakes in a new era with a powerful, ancient vampire who sets her sights on him.

https://books2read.com/Medallion

Golden Shackles – Book 3: When the ancient queen, Sekhmet snatches up Adam, he is faced with a terrifying decision. To help aid her in her vile plans or dare to stand against her.

https://books2read.com/GoldenShackles

In Gray

After a near fatal car crash brings Daisy Carmichael the ability to see the future, she is plagued by not only the things she sees, but the deadly secrets of the boy who saved her life.

https://books2read.com/InGray

Harvest Moon

Adeline Blackwood is a supernaturally gifted noble young woman who will do whatever is necessary to be with the man she loves. .

https://books2read.com/HarvestMoonBernhardt

Also from the Lavish family
_____

A New Life Series
Samantha Jacobey
https://www.lavishpublishing.com/authors/samantha-jacobey/

Bikers, rockers and the FBI clash in a dark, mature adult romantic thriller – Tori Farrell will go through hell to get her new life in a completed seven book series!

To what lengths would you go to break away from a life filled with pain and suffering?

Tori Farrell has lived a dangerous life. When you grow up with a Motorcycle Gang of Mercenaries and Drug Lords like the Dragons, a normal life is more like a fairytale. For years, she accepted her dark reality, a world consisting of drugs, sex, violence and murder. In the end, she learned the most valuable lesson: survival.

After years of being ruled by the Dragons, Tori uses her skills of seduction and assassination to free herself from the grasp of the people who vowed they would never let her go. Taken in by the FBI, she fears not everything is what it seems, and soon finds herself lost in a web of lies and deceit. She thought getting away from the Dragons would put her on a path to a new and better life, but now she must face the cold hard truth... there is always a price to be paid.

Sinister Series
A. Nicky Hjort
https://www.lavishpublishing.com/authors/nicky-hjort-1/

Thrillers that will take you to the edge and leave you breathless! Mature adult reads due to graphic sexual and violent material…

Sinister Bouquet: Awakening - Book 1: Devyn Mitchell has a choice… listen to the voice of her unborn baby – or die- again.

After a near death experience, Doctor Devyn Mitchell finds herself not only mysteriously pregnant but able to communicate with her fetus.

She has two choices: give in to total madness or surrender to her new reality, which just may be the only way she and her family will survive the obsessions of the Homeless Hunter's mind.

A true paranormal romantic thriller, A Sinister Bouquet: Awakening, the first of the Sinister Series, will take you right to the edge of what you know to be possible and then drop you in a place so dark, so terrifying, that the only passageway out is through the blinding light of awakening.

Wake up.
    Open your eyes.
    Finally.
    We've missed you so.

Sinister Vision: Know This Much Is True – Book 2: Elise Phillips, a doctor in training, has successfully repressed her kidnapping five years prior.

The only problem is...she has six and one half days to remember every terrible detail, or a total stranger will die. But to make matters even worse, in order to save this nameless woman, Elise will have to face something that scares her even more than death–intimacy.

Wake up. Open your eyes. Accept your assignment.
    ...The problem is not to find the answer–but to face it.

Know this much is true.